A tale of obsession

After a successful career as a designer with a fashion house which dressed the rich, royal and famous (remember Princess Diana's engagement sailor suit, and peach, going away outfit?), Richard Cawley swapped frocks for food when he won the Mouton Cadet cookery competition in *The Observer*. He has subsequently published nine cookbooks, numerous magazine and newspaper articles and become one of television's most popular chefs in such programmes as *Ready Steady Cook* and *Can't Cook Won't Cook*. He also teaches drawing and painting, runs a successful café and has starred in three pantomimes. However, a psychic in London and another in Sydney told him that he would write a successful novel. *The Butterfly Boy* was born ...

The Butterfly Boy Richard Cawley

First published 2000 by Millivres Ltd, part of the
Millivres Prowler Group, Gay Men's Press, PO Box 3220,
Brighton BN2 5AU, East Sussex, England

World Copyright © 2000 Richard Cawley

Richard Cawley has asserted his right to be identified
as the author of this work in accordance with the
Copyright, Designs and Patents Act 1988

THE FIRST TIME EVER I SAW YOUR FACE by Ewan MacColl
©Storming Music Inc, UK & Eire – Harmony Music Limited,
11 Uxbridge Street, London W8 7TQ.
All rights reserved. Used with permission.

A CIP catalogue record for this book is available
from the British Library

ISBN 1 902852 17 6

Distributed in Europe by Central Books,
99 Wallis Rd, London E9 5M

Distributed in North America by InBook/LPC Group,
1436 West Randolph, Chicago, IL 60607

Distributed in Australia by Bulldog Books,
PO Box 700, Beaconsfield, NSW 2014

Printed and bound in the EU by WS Bookwell, Juva, Finland

Photographer: Julien Trousselier
Model: Yuri Queiroz

THE BUTTERFLY BOY
Richard Cawley

For Michael

I would like to thank Chris, a psychic in London, Mary, a psychic in Sydney and an English Gypsy on Oxford Street, who all told me independently, within two months, that I should write this book.

I would like to thank Charlie for his invaluable help and encouragement with the initial stages of planning this story.

I would like to particularly thank the live butterfly which appeared and lived for several weeks in the bathroom of my rented house in Stevenage in January 1999 while I was appearing in pantomime. My mornings were free to write and one cold, grey morning, when I was suffering from a temporary lack of confidence, the butterfly mysteriously appeared and gave me the inspiration to continue.

I would mostly like to thank Andrew, my long-standing and long-suffering partner, for always being a tower of strength and encouraging me in every new project I have ever attempted.

Part I
Sydney, Australia

After the blistering February heat and late afternoon glare of the street, the dark doorway seemed at once both inviting and terrifying. For someone who had spent his life bravely coping with death, the dying, and the bereaved, it seemed insane to be afraid of climbing a flight of stairs to a cocktail bar, but somehow Janet Jackson's sexy invitation oozing down the stairs and past him into the street filled Michael with a feeling of faint terror. He pushed his rimless glasses nervously back up his nose and took a deep intake of breath.

David had never been keen on bars and clubs, and for the twelve years they had spent together, their almost obsessive love had all but obscured any world outside, except for the small, almost incestuous life of work at the charity. It was now just over a year since David had died and with deep feelings of guilt Michael had to admit to himself that at last the pain was subsiding a little, and the outside world was gradually beginning to insist on being noticed.

After the dark ascent, Gilligan's seemed shockingly bright and ordinary looking, Janet being the only one who was already in nightclub mode. The boys behind the bar looked fresh faced and bursting with good health as if they had just stepped out of the gym, which they most probably had.

Damian grinned from the other side of the room and thrust his arm towards Michael with an exaggerated thumbs up gesture. Michael paid for his drink, crossed the room and joined the others at their table by the open window, making a space for his bottle among the cocktail glasses, cigarette packets and mobile phones.

"Oh darl, trust you to be drinking beer, it's so boy, we're all doing Margaritas," Damian teased. "God, we'll never teach you to be a proper queer, will we girls? Now let's get to the business in hand, before we frighten you away. The big birthday."

"Oh god, no, please." Michael began to sweat.

"Darling you're not getting away with this one, tout Sydney is going to know that gorgeous Michael is about to turn forty."

"Please, please Damian, no, I just couldn't cope. Not yet, please."

"Don't panic darling," Mark butted in. "Even our dreadful Damian wouldn't be that cruel."

"Except for the full page ad. I've taken in the *Herald*," Damian continued. "No, seriously darling, we're only going to throw the teeniest bash for you, along the lines of an informal coronation. No, really, just us and the rest of the gang from work. A picnic in the park, and then we thought we might catch one of the outdoor movies. Kevin and Paul went last week and said it was totally fab."

Before Michael could protest he sensed a feeling of mild commotion and turned to see a tall skinny boy make 'an entrance' then move across the room from table to table, greeting and kissing almost everyone in the bar, and leaving behind him a wake of smiles and laughter and faces bright with obvious excitement. Everyone it seemed, knew, and apparently adored, this intriguing creature. At a table near the bar he crouched to share some obviously naughty snippet of gossip with a beautiful black clad girl with a blonde crew cut, swirling Celtic tattoos and numerous rings and studs in nose, lip, eyebrow and ears.

Like everyone else in the room Michael couldn't take his eyes of the boy as he crouched effortlessly, his spine and neck straight like a dancer's, his black wrap-around sunglasses on a level with the gorgeous blonde's identical ones making them appear like two exotic insects.

Fascinated, Michael silently dubbed him 'the Butterfly Boy' although, apart from the sunglasses, there was nothing really exotic or butterfly-like in the boy's clothing or appearance, or so it seemed at first sight. Tight black jeans, a skinny ribbed black tee shirt and black Nike trainers. His ink black hair was cut short and brushed forward in a spiky fringe.

Then with one sudden, flamboyant gesture the boy spun around to talk to someone at another table, at the same time removing his sunglasses to reveal eyes of the most startling brilliant blue. Until then, Michael realised, he had only seen the boy's left hand side. In the perfect lobe of that perfect right ear something shone which sent a shiver down Michael's spine. One small earring, brilliantly enamelled and in the shape of a butterfly.

"Goodness me darling, something *has* caught your attention. I wouldn't have imagined that'd be your type! Surely you're not beginning to join the real world are you?" Damian jibed.

The heavy black, oh so familiar feelings immediately surged back, making Michael's body feel like lead, his stomach instantly knotting itself. But now a new feeling was added to these tireless companions, a feeling of creeping guilt.

Anyway, the boy couldn't be older than nineteen or twenty, and although Michael knew that he was good looking, handsome even, in a rather boring kind of way, a boy like that would never give him a second thought. Surely? Nevertheless it made him a little uneasy when the boy sat down and joined a crowd of yet more gorgeous young things at the next table.

"Michael I do believe you're blushing. Now come on, let's get down to the business in hand. This might be a teeny, casual affair, but these things have to be planned to the last detail. I mean we don't want everyone turning up with the same quiche, in fact my sweet we don't want anyone at all turning up with quiche. So ordinaire darling. So very common."

After half an hour of Damian's non-stop party prattle, punctuated by lewd or cutting remarks about every new person who entered the bar, Michael began to feel better, light hearted almost. Thank god for friends, especially kind hearted silly queens like Damian. Michael found himself actually laughing at the ridiculous conversation.

"No darling we don't need eskies, we'll just buy loads and loads of icy cold bubbly from the bottle shop on the way to the bash. It won't be in the bottles long enough to get warm darl! You can bring an eski if you like sweetie but remember you'll be stuck with it all night. I suppose it wouldn't matter at the movies, but would you really want to take it on to The Rat Club. I suppose we could all dance round it and pretend it was the very latest Prada handbag. Just think darls, before you knew it every queen in Sydney would be carrying one. Now who do I have to fuck around here to get a drink?"

Michael stood and turned to go to the bar.

"Well, I know I've no chance of the fuck, you gorgeous man, but I won't say no to another Margarita. I'll have a frozen one this time, and tell that bar bitch not to forget the fucking salt this time."

As he stood at the bar watching a beautiful muscular boy going through the performance of mixing cocktails, a soft voice almost whispered into Michael's left ear.

"Did I hear the 'P' word ?"

He spun round and felt himself blush. The butterfly flashed rainbow colours in the light. The boy's eyes, close to, were so intensely blue, they were almost unreal. And a new sensation. A slightly exotic perfume, faint enough to be almost unnoticeable, but decidedly exotic.

"The 'P' word?" Michael just managed to stutter.

"Party, darling, party. I adore parties. What's it for? Can I come?"

"It's for my ...birthday, but I really don't think you'd enjoy it. It's not going to be anything special. Just a picnic. Just us really." Michael turned and nodded towards the table by the window, where all eyes were on him. He felt another blush rising. "Everyone's bringing some food, and I'm bringing some champagne, and then we're going to see an outdoor movie. *Some Like it Hot*, I think."

"Sounds divine darling. Well?"

"Well what?"

"Well you haven't answered my question."

"What question?"

"Can I come?"

"Well, yes," Michael stammered again. "I suppose so if you think you wouldn't be bored. We're meeting on Thursday, oh that's tomorrow isn't it, on the steps of the Art Gallery at six thirty."

"I'll be there, and I promise not to be bored. I definitely won't be bored!"

The boy stared straight into Michael's eyes at the same time giving him a boyish little punch on the shoulder. Michael dropped his head to hide his obvious delight and yet another blush. By the time he looked up he was just in time to see the straight skinny back in the black ribbed tee shirt disappearing out of the door. Janet Jackson was singing again, unaware of the importance of the moment, her voice following the boy down the stairs and out of the door.

※

Of the fifteen birthday cards ranged on the mantelpiece, eleven bore identical hand written messages.

'Nobody loves a fairy when she's forty.' How typical. Queens! But fifteen cards, nevertheless. Michael felt a warm, almost cosy feeling, followed immediately by a wave of butterflies in the stomach as he thought of the evening to come. He smiled a little as he realised the irony of the butterfly connection.

The Butterfly Boy

"I don't know how long we're all supposed to wait for the little princess. She's over ten minutes late, the grog's getting warm, and I can't wait to get stuck into the sushi, not to mention Kevin's divine looking rocket salad darlings," Damian almost screeched. "Oh Michael don't look so horrified! It's your party and of course we'll wait for your new *petit amour*."

Before Michael could react, a taxi screeched to a halt. Michael watched the boy hand some money to the woman driver and wait for the change. She seemed to be greatly amused. Her fat body shook with laughter. The boy leapt out, ran straight up to Michael and thrust a single red rose into his hand. "Sorry," he grinned.

"It's fine, absolutely fine. You didn't need to."

"Don't worry darling, I stole it from a table outside a restaurant." The boy tossed back his head and laughed. Michael suspected it to be true.

The party was lovely. Quite low key and gentle. There was lots of laughter, but even Damian for once, seemed to realise that now was the time to hold back.

In turn, everyone came to talk to Michael, and, Michael noticed, not one person mentioned his age. Michael felt an overwhelming gush of love for all his friends. How sweet they were to be so tactful.

The boy sat close to Michael on a plastic carrier bag which had held champagne. Obviously to protect the immaculate white jeans. He seemed quite different from the butterfly creature of the evening before. Quite quiet and attentive, answering Michael's questions briefly with a soft gentle voice which seemed to caress Michael's body like countless warm tongues. He was older than Michael had thought. Twenty two. Michael supposed that made it a bit better? He was in his second year of the fashion design course at East Sydney Tech and shared a house in Paddington with three other fashion students. Michael felt relieved when he discovered they were all girls. But how ridiculous, he thought, to be feeling possessive and jealous. He turned to look at the boy, who was now talking to Mark. He looked so beautiful, so perfect. His simply, white clad body, unadorned except for the enamelled butterfly.

Oh, god, thought Michael, this is such a mistake, but it's too late.

Night was beginning to fall as they dumped the picnic debris into the bins. Eager possums peered down, unseen, from the gum trees, anticipating the rich, and decidedly chic pickings.

A mellow champagne-induced feeling pervaded the little party as they ambled down the hill, through the park to the water's edge, where the sun was putting on a show of spectacular vulgarity, as it disappeared behind the Bridge and the Opera House, as if in protest at having to miss all the fun to come.

Michael hung back, walking a few paces behind Sean and Dan. Mark, who had been the last to leave the picnic spot, typically ensuring that no one had left so much as a cigarette end or champagne cork behind, overtook him, giving him a playful little cuff on the back of the head and walked quickly on to join Damian. The boy walked silently beside Michael. Oh god, he's bored stiff, Michael agonised silently. I'm just too old to be having these crazy emotions about some unknown boy I've just met. But I suppose he could go and join some of the younger ones if he was that bored, he consoled himself.

The guy selling the tickets for the movie smiled a 'Goodness you're gorgeous, where-have-you-been-all-my-life, lets-shag-here-and-now' look at Michael. "Fourteen dollars a ticket." His eyes lowered for a split second and then back up to Michael's with a barely perceptible widening, as if to say 'Slip me your phone number on the way out.' Michael knew that everyone must get the same treatment from this little 'actor', but it nevertheless pleased him and gave him the little bit of extra confidence he needed to really enjoy the evening. He suddenly felt attractive and hoped the boy had noticed the small flirtation. Disappointingly he hadn't, but was fumbling in his pockets.

"Don't worry," said Michael. "Two please."

"Thanks," said the boy almost sheepishly.

The party boys were all sitting together in the second row from the front. The end seat and the one next to it had been tactfully left free for Michael and the boy. Mark was in the third seat and Michael slid in next to him leaving the end seat for the boy, who hesitated and said

"Drink? I noticed there's a bar. Shall I get us one before the movie starts?"

Michael went to put his hand in his pocket, but the boy, laughing, was gone.

Michael could feel Mark looking at him and with a small involuntary sigh turned to see his best friend's face filled with concern.

"Michael do be careful. You're such an old softie, don't get serious, this is not the boy to fall in love with. He's nice enough, but I'm sure he's just playing with you, you'll only get hurt."

"Of course I won't get serious, I'm old enough to know better than to fall for a butterfly like that!" He wished he hadn't used the word. "I'm just amusing myself for the evening."

"Michael my dear, dear friend, I've known you for long enough to recognise when you're lying, you were always hopeless at it! Well just be careful and remember, when you want a shoulder to cry on, that your faithful old buddy is just in the apartment across the landing, as usual, with a cup of tea and a sympathetic ear."

Michael grinned, in acknowledgement of his innermost feelings being so transparent, and his eyes welled with tears of affection for this faithful friend who he had known since his art school days. A friend who'd seen him through thick and thin, and there had certainly been plenty of both in the last couple of years leading up to David's death.

Suddenly an icy beer was thrust into his hand, and to the accompaniment of an almost deafening trumpet fanfare, the biggest screen Michael had ever seen rose majestically from the surface of the harbour. As the first images flashed across the screen, a group of bats swooped and wheeled in front of the picture as if revelling in the brilliantly moving shafts of light. The previously dominant skyline of the city, now paled into a shadowy background, except for a splattering of tiny specks of light from the millions of high rise windows.

The film which Michael had already seen many times

before was nevertheless still funny and charming, but the boy, who had never seen it, was obviously enchanted, nudging Michael frequently and laughing uproariously. In between nudges, Michael's mind drifted constantly from the movie as he agonised over his new emotions. He hadn't felt quite like this since he was fifteen and had a huge and all consuming crush on an older boy at school. How ridiculous he felt, but at the same time the feeling brought with it a certain excitement. He allowed himself to wallow in the presence of this wild crazy boy sitting so close, next to him. How could he see him again? He must. How could he have him just to himself, if only for a short while? Perhaps he could persuade him to come to the country for the weekend. But no, he was obviously such a city boy, a party animal. He'd be bored stiff, and he'd never understand the shack. Besides how could he take another boy there when it had been so special to David? And yet he knew that if it was at all possible he would. He also knew that in his present state of infatuation, he probably wouldn't even feel guilty, well, perhaps a little. He had only been back to the shack a couple of times since the funeral.

Michael's reverie was suddenly halted. The movie was over, everyone was clapping, and beginning to edge out of their seats.

"Did you enjoy it?" Michael asked.

"I adored it. What next?"

Michael was taken aback. " I hadn't really thought."

"Well it's too early to go dancing!"

Michael felt a feeling of growing panic. He hadn't been to a nightclub for years, and even then he had always been a terrible dancer, but he couldn't say he didn't want to go?

"Let's drop in at Number Twelve, for another cocktail or two." the boy continued "and then we only have to fall across the street into Amnesia!"

The last of the birthday party revellers drifted off, after happy birthday, good-bye kisses and knowing looks. All Michael's friends were desperately hoping that at last he was going to emerge from his terrible period of black grieving. Michael flashed a look back to Kevin, the last to say good-bye, as if to say 'help' but Kevin just grinned and walked away with the others, disappearing into the park, laughing and joking.

Michael felt very alone and inadequate. He had never even heard of Number Twelve. It turned out to be one of the traditional Sydney corner pubs, which until quite recently had been frequented by local Darlinghurst 'characters' - hard drinking men and even harder drinking women - but was now stripped out, decorated in chrome, concrete and blonde wood and frequented by a younger, trendier crowd. Michael felt oddly conspicuous dressed in his blue checked shirt, because, boring as it was, it was the only splash of colour in this totally monochrome environment. Every other person drinking in the bar seemed to be dressed entirely in black and grey, except of course for the butterfly boy, who stood out in his still immaculate whites.

Michael bought a Hahn Premium beer for himself, and a Stoli and lemonade for the boy, who once again was turning what had been a rather sober crowd into an instant party as he flitted from group to group, kissing almost everyone in the bar, once more leaving laughter and smiles at every table.

The Butterfly Boy

As soon as Michael moved to sit at the only remaining empty table however, the boy immediately rejoined him, once again quiet and attentive. The obvious attention and the alcohol gave Michael a sudden burst of courage and he blurted.

"I've got a little place in the country, not much, a shack really. I'm driving up on Friday night for the weekend. You wouldn't, I mean, I don't suppose, you'd, well, like to come, I mean, there is nothing to do, you'd probably hate it, no, forget it, really."

"Shhh." The boy shut Michael up with one slim forefinger held gently against his lips. " I'd love to Michael." The first time he had called Michael by his name. Michael's heart was suddenly beating so loudly, he was sure everyone in the bar could hear it.

"Oh dear, there's a bit of a prob, though, I'm afraid. You couldn't wait until Saturday to drive up, could you? I've got an important fitting in the morning for our big fashion show. I can't miss it, the show's going to be a huge affair, circus tent in Victoria Park. It's sponsored by Coca-Cola. They're *throwing* money at us, it's going to be so lavish, the event of the season, and guess who's doing the finale? *Moi,* darling, a mere second year. The third year are absolutely livid. You must come, tickets are bar gold, but I'll get you one. You will come won't you? ... Don't you just love this? It's the new Madonna."

It took Michael a minute to realise that the boy had changed the subject and was now talking about the music. Everything was suddenly moving too fast. Could he believe it? Had the boy really said that he would come to the country with him? Wait until Saturday? He would wait a week, a month, anything just to be with this amazing glittering creature again.

Michael went to the bar to get more drinks, but this time the boy asked for mineral water. Out of the corner of his eye Michael watched the boy talking to another of about the same age who had just appeared in the doorway of the bar, silhouetted against a brilliant rectangle provided by a nearby street lamp. Michael watched as something obviously passed from hand to hand. The new boy disappeared from the rectangle of light and the butterfly disappeared in the direction of the men's room.

Michael hated himself for being so irritated by the smoky atmosphere of Rat Club. It wasn't nearly as scary as he had anticipated, and so what if his clothes smelt in the morning, they could go straight in the wash. The music certainly wasn't to his normal taste, but somehow the constant throbbing beat was becoming quite addictive, and he found that he didn't mind what people thought about his dancing. Beer in hand, he couldn't stop. Was he the only one drinking alcohol? Why were all these kids just drinking water? How many beers had he had? Oh, what the hell, this was fun, where was the boy? Oh over there, flitting from flower to flower as usual, but what the hell, he was going to spend the weekend with him. Michael suddenly felt such a surge of joy and excitement, that he felt like turning a cartwheel. Not that he had ever done something as extrovert as that, but the thought suddenly made him realise that he was really very drunk indeed. He heard his voice sounding slightly slurred as he ordered yet another beer, and found the bar a very welcome support. It felt sticky. Michael looked at his watch. His thoughts, feelings, felt at the same time blurred and yet heightened, exaggerated, noticeable! Michael looked at his watch, and when he eventually managed to focus on it, he saw that it was already almost three a.m. He turned, holding himself upright, by leaning heavily with his waist against the bar. He felt weirdly conscious of his belt digging into his waist. He tried to focus on the dancers, those gorgeous young things looked, so, well, gorgeous.

A single figure appeared to separate itself from the throbbing crowd. It seemed to be getting bigger, coming closer. Michael blinked to try and clear his vision. It was definitely coming closer, dancing towards him.

A boy, young, very young? Difficult to tell without seeing his eyes. Sunglasses, wrap-around, insect-like, silver. The boy grinned as he 'performed' for Michael. Blonde hair, short, brushed forward, like the butterfly boy. Where is he? I'll look for him later. Baggy khaki fatigues, suspended from narrow hips. A band of white Calvin Klein's, then a gyrating torso shining, golden, hairless. A ring in the perfect neat naval, decorated with a green coloured stone, flashed as the boy writhed, snake-like to the incredibly loud frenzied music. The nipples, Michael noticed, were tiny, like two brown cake crumbs. Whilst the body continued its sinuous, sensual movements, the slender arms thrashed about almost violently, flashing at incredible speed this way and that, crossing and circling, to the sides and the front, and above his head, but never lower than chest height. The armpits, smooth and hairless like those of a child. He danced close enough for Michael to smell his perfume, then whisked off his sunglasses and laughed.

His eyes! Yellow with a lozenge shaped pupil, like an animal, a cat! The boy laughed again and stuck out his tongue, inches from Michael's face. He quivered it, pierced, a large metal stud. Michael shuddered. The boy laughed once more then span and was gone, dissolved back into the crowd.

Michael turned back towards the bar and caught sight of himself in the mirror. Not only did he feel drunk, uncomfortably so now, boringly so, but he realised he also looked it! Or did he look drunk because he felt drunk? His thoughts, he realised, were getting as slurred as his speech.

Although Michael had always had very conservative views about drugs, of all kind, the sight of all these beautiful young people, dancing with such wild energy, but still so fresh looking, so pleasant, so fabulous, began to put a different complexion on things. He would, he decided, think about it tomorrow. Tomorrow! Oh god. Tomorrow. Wasn't he meeting the boy tomorrow? Yes, outside the Albury, not till twelve. But what day was tomorrow? Oh what a relief. Tomorrow was only Friday, not Saturday. Michael felt ridiculously proud of that particular piece of mental agility. Perhaps he wasn't as drunk as he thought he was? He edged his body slightly away from the bar just to test this theory. His confidence faltered as he realised how unsteady on his feet he was.

He turned slightly sideways to pick up his bottle, for 'just one last drink' when he discovered there was already another hand around the bottle! They both laughed. The hand belonged to a face. A slightly blurred face, but a blurred laughing face. A blurred, laughing, handsome face. A blurred, laughing, handsome, friendly, sexy face! About the same age as him, Michael guessed. Handsome but decidedly rough looking.

The Butterfly Boy

Deeply rutted 'laugh' lines ran vertically down either side of a too thin, but decidedly sexy mouth. Cruel, but humorous, dark, almost black eyes, which drifted in and out of focus, spelled sex, raw, rough, all consuming, fun sex! No holds barred sex. Fuck tomorrow sex. Oh god!

"OK, let's share it."

The words came from the thin lips. Michael managed to focus as he watched the guy tip back his head and empty the remains of the beer into his mouth. A vein throbbed in his lean tanned, slightly bristly neck. Michael felt slightly unreal. Not-in-control. He knew he was going to feel like hell in the morning. Remorse? What would he remember. Oh god! The beautiful young people danced in continued frenzy, fresh faced, smiling, oh shit why wouldn't his eyes focus, where was the boy, his boy, his butterfly boy? The guy standing next to him at the bar suddenly grabbed Michael's head, a rough hand over each ear, he smashed his mouth onto Michael's, forced his lips open with an unbelievably muscular and agile tongue, and squirted warm beer down Michael's throat.

"Well, I said let's share it." The guy grinned and swayed unsteadily.

Michael felt his entrails dissolving into what felt like a stomach full of soup. His cock instantly hardened. He felt his jeans would rip apart. He had to escape!

Somehow, he had somehow managed to get himself home. Next day he was amazed, he certainly couldn't remember how. By taxi? Key? Yes! Credit cards? Yes. Thank god. Surprisingly when he woke at six a.m. and got up for a pee, after only three hours sleep, he had no hangover! He felt wonderful in fact, in love with the world. In love with the butterfly boy?

A shower? Yes a shower, that was the answer! Had there been a question? Michael felt mad, but then realised that he was actually still drunk. What the hell, he felt wonderful. He couldn't remember when he had felt so elated. He could fly, yes if he really wanted to he could fly. But he didn't need to. He would save that. Meanwhile a shower. Yes a shower. He put *Handel Suites for Keyboard* on the CD player. Keith Jarret seemed to imbue the music with a haunting modern touch. Almost jazzy, he loved it. He turned it up loud, sod the neighbours. When had he ever upset the neighbours? When had he ever been, even slightly, badly behaved?

He threw his head back in the shower. Luxuriated, revelled in the rather too hot water. He opened his mouth and allowed the hot foaming water to fill it, overflow, he wished it was beer. He remembered. He laughed. Then for a moment a split second feeling of panic. Would he turn up on Saturday? The boy? His boy? The butterfly boy? His butterfly boy? Was he just playing games? Yes? No? Michael felt just too wonderful, too elated to doubt, to care. He felt he could fly. Oh god. He realised that he was actually still very drunk, and he had to be at work, sensible, in a couple of hours. Breakfast. Yes, that would help. He opened the sliding mirrored door of his wardrobe. Oh god, I am so boring, he thought, as he looked at a neat row of almost identical, perfectly ironed blue checked shirts. A pile of perfectly pressed denim jeans, another of beige shorts, and another of pristine, carefully folded white tee shirts.

The coffee shop on the Military Road, was like so many others, blonde wood, rack of newspapers and magazines to read, a relaxed, clubby neighbourhood atmosphere. Excellent food. Michael was suddenly aware of how great it was to live in Sydney. It was so easy, so comfortable, so civilised. A bright eyed young girl took his order. A freshly squeezed juice. Carrot and orange with a hint of fresh ginger. Then one poached egg, mushrooms, grilled tomatoes and brown toast, a skimmed milk latte. Just ordering what would be such an enjoyable, healthy breakfast made Michael begin to feel more down to earth, grown up. But the new feeling of excitement, elation, ebullience, he mentally tried to find a word to describe it adequately, kept welling up. Once more he had the feeling that he could fly. He almost ran back home after breakfast. As if it would make tomorrow come quicker.

Mark stepped out of the lift just as Michael opened the glass doors into the lobby of their small block of apartments.

"My goodness Michael you look like the cat that got the cream. Obviously not home-alone last night?"

"No, no," Michael protested. But then with a faintly smug smile he added, "But he is coming to the country with me at the weekend."

"What are you like?" Mark shrilled in a mock camp voice. "No, seriously darling," his voice back to familiar warm, best buddy tones, "just have the best time. You deserve it. And I know it's pointless saying it but be careful, don't get in too deep, don't get hurt. I'm the one that will have to pick up the pieces and try and put you back together again!"

Mark jogged off. Lean and clean, as always, Michael thought as Mark headed in the direction of the Military Road for his habitual morning exercise.

Dear old Mark, Michael mused affectionately. All the time I've known him he's never had a long term relationship. It's such a shame, he's so kind, and capable and affectionate. He would make some lucky boy so happy.

That night after work, Michael went up to Woollies to shop for food for the weekend, well, half a weekend. He wanted it to be perfect though. The food must be delicious, but simple. He was a good cook, but he didn't want it to look like he was showing off. Neither did he want to spend other than the minimum of time cooking when they got to the shack. He bought some baby green beans and some pine kernels for a first course salad. Then some fresh raw prawns to cook in butter with garlic and lots of parsley, to serve on pasta. Lots of fresh fruit, several kinds of bread, eggs and other stuff for breakfast.

Another shop behind Woolworth's made the best fresh pasta ever. Then a stop off at the bottle shop. A selection of really good wines, plus champagne, French champagne. This had to be perfect. On the one hand he didn't want the boy to realise, well not yet, that since David had died, he had become really quite rich. But there again he did want him to feel rather spoilt and pampered. So that being with Michael decidedly had its advantages!

Back in the apartment, in his immaculate little, white and stainless steel kitchen, where everything had its place, and nothing was out of place; he blanched the beans and toasted the pine kernels for the salad. Then he made a dressing with his best, ridiculously expensive estate bottled extra virgin olive oil, a little very good balsamic vinegar, pepper and a pinch of Maldon salt. This was made in a screw topped jar, ready for transportation. Everything was carefully planned to the last detail. All except the food and wines in the fridge everything was very soon ready, packed to go in the car, and it wasn't even seven o'clock yet! There was nothing on tv. Should he go over and see if Mark felt like going out for some Thai food? No, he certainly didn't feel like a lecture on being careful and not getting too emotional. For once in his life he didn't feel sensible at all, and he was enjoying it. There was a new French film on at the Hayden Orpheum. He would walk up the road and see it to fill the time and occupy his mind.

🦋

Saturday eventually came. Michael woke before six. It was going to be a very hot day. He drove down to the swimming pool at North Sydney to kill more time and burn of some energy.

By twelve, the agreed hour, terrified of being late Michael had driven around several blocks, several times. At last he drove slowly along Oxford Street from the City end. The cafés were all full of late breakfasters, sipping their lattes, skinnycinos and fresh juices, and gossiping lazily over the papers.

The day was hot, very hot, but with almost no humidity. The air seemed to fizz and sparkle like champagne, albeit hot champagne. Once again Michael experienced the strange feeling that, if he tried, he could fly. Oh god, there he was, standing almost in the gutter, a huge black portfolio in one hand, a small black back pack slung over one shoulder. Toothbrush? Michael was almost sick with excitement.

A mobile phone was wedged between the boy's ear and a skinny shoulder. The conversation was obviously amusing. "How can I ever compete?" Michael agonised. "But he has turned up. Oh god he looks even more gorgeous than ever!" A tight ribbed white tee shirt, tucked into baggy beige cotton shorts, which hung around his narrow hips and ended exactly in the middle of his tanned knees. A pair of sunglasses tucked into the shallow V of the tee shirt. Very simple black Nike trainers and thick white cotton socks crumpled down over his ankles. The exposed portion of slender shin and calf, a perfect coppery gold, shimmered with a haze of surprisingly blonde fine hairs. On his oh-so-perfectly shaped, neat head, a white cotton baseball cap with the words Country Road embroidered discreetly in white across the front. He looked so clean, so boyish, so wholesome, except for the flower! A single frangipani blossom, white with a yellow centre, was tucked behind one ear. Not the ear with the butterfly. That was hidden behind the phone; it was however, Michael saw with delight, when the phone moved slightly, still in place.

"Bye darl," the boy laughed down the phone, jumping into the car, and throwing his portfolio over onto the back seat. "Hello, Michael," he grinned cheekily, folding away his phone, and struggling out of his ruck sack and into his seat belt. "That was Meera on the phone. She's choreographing the show. She's totally fab. We're so lucky to have her, she doesn't need the work, she's only doing it as a favour to Travis, Travis who runs the course, they're old friends, right back to the sixties apparently, though Travis would die rather than admit he was old enough to have been around in the sixties, but he was. I know he studied fashion under Janey Ironside at the Royal College, he *is* proud of that, I checked the dates!"

For the next two hours as they drove north through the scorching midday heat, windows open in preference to air con, the boy chatted incessantly, mostly about the coming fashion show. Michael listened, fascinated, silent for the most part. This boy, this wonderful, beautiful, adorable boy, was obviously not merely a butterfly, nor merely a creature of the night, but, it was becoming more and more obvious, was seemingly talented, and totally passionate about his work. Michael thrilled at this new revelation. If he was a worker, perhaps he was a settler? Michael desperately hoped so. He was falling totally and hopelessly in love. Mentally he had already pushed his own clothes to one side of the wardrobe! Yet there had been nothing whatsoever to suggest that the boy felt anything at all in return. There *had* been the rose, but it *had* been his birthday, and save for a playful punch and a finger placed momentarily on his lips, there had been no physical contact whatsoever.

Twice the boy's phone rang, and each time the caller was politely but decisively cut short. Michael was thrilled, flattered, elated. The being-able-to-fly sensation grew stronger and stronger. He was glad he had decided to take the back road instead of the highway, even though it put over an hour on the journey. It was so quiet. They had hardly seen another car, and it meant that they could stop at Anita's for a late lunch . But most of all, it meant another hour alone with the butterfly boy, so close. Michael turned sideways to devour him with his eyes. He was on the phone again! How could a seat belt be sexy? Yet Michael could hardly bear to look at it, wrapped around that skinny, almost non-existent torso. How he wished he could replace the nylon strap with his hungry arms. Oh god. How would he know when? Would he ever dare to make a move? He mustn't rush things. He mustn't fuck everything up. Yet, how he longed to hold him, to crush him, to crush the breath out of him. To silence the incessant chatter with a kiss, to smother every inch of that slender willowy body in kisses. This butterfly creature, so apparently free with his own kisses, yet strangely distant, well behaved, almost shy, with Michael. For the first time Michael allowed himself to imagine what it would actually feel like to kiss that mouth. He felt quite faint. The crotch of his jeans felt uncomfortably tight. Oh god, he thought with a little embarrassment, but a certain amount of delight. How long has it been since anyone gave me a stiffy? Then he remembered the guy in the club, the beer! He smiled inwardly.

Just as the situation was beginning to be embarrassing, they drove over the brow of a small hill. Suddenly in solitary splendour, there was Anita's, a seedy looking service station, set a little back from the road, corrugated tin roof, white peeling paint and three petrol pumps. A blue heeler, lay panting under one of the two dilapidated wooden benches, which ran along the front of the building on either side of the central door. They parked to the side of the building, in the relative shade of a large gum tree, between an extraordinarily weather-beaten 'ute' and a brand new white Toyota four wheel drive. In the back of the Toyota, on one side, hung a black dinner suit, complete with starched white shirt, on the other side something dark, under a polythene bag.

The Butterfly Boy

"Mmmm, how chic, Donna Karan, the real thing!" muttered the boy, peering indiscreetly into the window. "The bush can't be that boring Michael!" he smirked. The third time he had spoken Michael's name!

As they pushed their way through the greasy multicoloured plastic ribbons of the door curtain, the Toyota owners were just coming out. They smiled openly. A perfect golden couple. Rich country kids, Michael mentally surmised. The boy, tall, blonde, athletic, not more than twenty years old, simply oozed good health, and money. His streaky blonde hair, pushed behind his ears, reached almost to his broad bulky shoulders. A faint splattering of freckles, stopped his high wide cheekbones and chiselled nose looking too perfect. His faded Mambo board shorts, singlet, and bare feet, intended to signify cool beach bum merely emphasised the fact that he was obviously a highly privileged rich kid, with never so much as a hint of a cloud on the horizon.

The girl was an equally splendid specimen of gilded youth. Tall lean body, clad in pristine white cotton. What was it about these kids, and their seeming abhorrence of colour? Michael thought, conscious of his checked shirt. She wore perfectly plain shorts, tee shirt and tennis shoes. Her blonde hair hung heavy and straight, almost to her shoulder blades, unbelievably shiny, like spun glass, in the harsh sunlight. In one hand she held a large burger, The works. Anita was justly famous for her burgers, and although she looked like the worst kind of trailer park slut, everything she served was home made, and tasted wonderful. The juice from the beetroot was beginning to leak over the golden girl's perfect hand. Would it dare to stain any of those immaculate, expensive white clothes? In the other hand she carried a white baseball cap; one finger hooked under the adjustable back strap.

Anita joked with Michael, pleased to see him obviously more cheerful, as she cooked their burgers. She related an extraordinarily filthy joke about transvestites and anchovies. Her enormously fat body shook grotesquely with laughter inside the giant tube of printed polyester which gripped her under sweating arm pits on too-tight elastic. Then, when the laughter had subsided and the boy was momentarily distracted, flicking through the pages of *The Land* in a disinterested fashion, she flashed Michael a "So-what's-all-this-about?" look. Michael blushed, shrugged his shoulders and grinned sheepishly as he paid for the food.

As they leant on the car, under the tree, to escape from the fierce sunshine, the flies, Michael noticed, which were attacking him from all sides, weren't bothering the boy at all. The boy's tee shirt, Michael also observed, still looked freshly ironed and was completely dry, whereas his own was completely stuck to him with sweat. Was the boy enchanted? Michael certainly was with him.

The rich kids sat on one of the wooden benches, in the narrow ribbon of shadow provided by the overhanging tin roof, obviously perfectly happy in each other's company, so relaxed, so easy with each other. Michael was envious. The boy gave the remains of his burger to the dog, whose tail indicated the double pleasure of being fed, and at the same time having the golden boy's naked toes wriggling into the grey hairs of his belly. The girl got up first, stretching. She threw the debris of her meal into the rusting rubbish bin, sending up a cloud of flies. Michael noticed that she too seemed unbothered by the stifling heat. She suddenly bent forward from the waist, so that her perfect hair fell almost to the ground, and with one quick dextrous movement, she twisted it onto the top of her head and secured it in place with the white baseball cap.

Michael was surprised, although he knew he shouldn't have been when she got into the drivers seat. He then turned and saw her companion disappear once more through the greasy plastic ribbons.

"I'll get us some cold drinks for the car," said the butterfly boy, collecting up the rubbish, which he dropped in the bin, again disturbing the flies, and then he too was swallowed up by the plastic ribbons.

Michael smiled as he watched through the window. He wished he had the confidence and ability to be able to talk to everyone like that. A roaring belly laugh from Anita, momentarily drowned the incessant electric hum of the cicadas. He compared the two boys, so very different, one so dark, slight and feline, almost feminine; the other so big and golden, so open, and boyish. They seemed to be having a pleasant chat. The butterfly seemed quite addicted to people, he seemed to need to talk to everyone. To win them over. Was he compensating for something? Was he maybe not as confident and sure of himself as he seemed? If so he did a remarkable show of hiding it.

After what seemed like ages, the two boys emerged from the building and walked together, still chatting towards the cars. Then after lad-ish "See yer mates" they got into their respective vehicles. Michael started the engine and laughed as his boy proffered a large opened bag of jelly snakes.

The white Toyota disappeared down the road in front of them in a huge cloud of dust. The afternoon heat was almost unbearable, and the bottle of cold Mount Franklin water was more than welcome. Michael thrilled to share it with the boy, drinking from the bottle. He noticed that the boy never bothered to wipe the neck of the bottle after Michael had drunk from it. He was flattered and found it more than a little erotic.

"How long have you had this shack?" the boy asked.

Michael explained how, just after David had been diagnosed positive, a wealthy uncle of his had died and left him everything, and for Christmas three years ago David had bought Michael the shack as a Christmas present.

"We christened it the shack, but it's really just a fibro, two bedroomed single story cottage . It originally only had one bedroom, but at some stage the occupants boxed in the front veranda with fibro panels and frosted glass to provide another one. It's quite interesting because it was designed in the twenties as a staff cottage. You see next door there's a huge nineteenth century mansion, Riverlands, which was originally built by a rich family called the Greens. In fact it's still lived in by the Green family. Riverlands is surrounded by huge sprawling grounds and the shack was originally right on the edge. Then it was sold off in the thirties and fenced off with its own little block of land. The old guy who lived their, moved up to live with his daughter in Queensland when his wife died, so David bought it off him lock stock and barrel.

The boy seemed interested, smiling and nodding but the

heat was obviously making him sleepy.

They drove in silence for another half hour or so. The boy jerked his head from its slumped position, waking himself up. He turned to Michael and giggled. Then, without speaking he turned on the cassette player in the dashboard. The tape had been there, undisturbed, for well over a year. Michael swerved, braking violently, leaving great curved black tyre marks on the road and nearly turning the car over onto the dry grass verge. Michael had completely forgotten about the tape. His hand scrabbled wildly at the controls, his eyes blinded with floods of scalding unstoppable tears. But, before he could silence her, Roberta Flack had already sung too much of the poignant `The first time ever I saw your face.'

Michael struggled with the car door, then threw it open, fell out, ran stumbling a few yards ahead, then fell to his knees. His head in his hands, tears running through his fingers and falling as heavy drops into the burning dust and splattering his glasses where they had fallen. His shoulders shook so hard that the boy, who had followed him, thought perhaps he must be ill or having some kind of fit. "Michael. What's the matter, what is it?" The boy's voice was filled with obvious panic. He put one concerned hand on Michael's back, picking up the mercifully undamaged glasses with the other. The radiant heat from the flesh beneath the wet tee shirt, and the violent shrug of rejection gave the boy the sensation that he had actually been physically burned. He took a couple of steps back and then stood there helpless and genuinely afraid. What could he possibly have done to have provoked such a violent reaction in this gentle, quiet man? Then the realisation hit him like a sledge hammer. The song. Oh no. It must have been 'their song'. Yes, it was obviously their song.

"Oh Michael, I'm so sorry. How could I possibly have known?"

This time Michael didn't shrug away his hand. He just bent forward even more so that his forehead now touched the ground. The boy crouched on one knee beside him, his hand resting hot and uncomfortably in the middle of Michael's back. It felt heavy and awkward, but it seemed to be having some effect. The convulsive sobbing was at last gradually subsiding. The hard gritty ground bit into the boy's knee. But he didn't move. He gripped the thin gold arm of the glasses tightly lest they fall to the ground again. Minutes passed. He plucked up the courage and hooked the hand that had been on Michael's back around one shoulder, standing himself, and gently pulling Michael upright.

"Come on, we can't stay like this. Come back to the car. I'd offer to drive, but, well, I can't drive!"

"It's OK. I'm fine now. I'll be alright. Honestly. Look I'm really, really sorry. You see, that song..." The tears started again.

"Don't explain, I understand." The boy pulled his tee shirt out from his shorts, carefully cleaned the glasses and handed them back to Michael, who slowly put them on after wiping his eyes awkwardly with the back of his hand.

"No, I want to. Do you mind if we go and sit over there in the shade for a while? I still feel a bit shaky, I don't feel up to driving just yet."

The boy fetched the remains of the bottle of water, now warm, and followed Michael to sit on a fallen tree.

The Butterfly Boy

It was the boy's turn to listen. Michael talked quietly, calmly and steadily for over an hour. The boy was silent. Just nodding occasionally. He was obviously moved by the whole story. The meeting, falling in love, the happy years together followed by the unhappy years, the awful all pervasive all consuming sickness. The dying. The grieving. The terrible depression. The loneliness.

But suddenly Michael didn't feel lonely any more. The feeling of wanting to fly came surging back. He had never really talked like this to anyone about the whole thing. Not even to Mark, his best friend. The feeling of relief was overwhelming. His body felt lighter. His head felt clearer. He straightened his back and turned to look at the boy for the first time since he had started talking. Oh god, how beautiful he looks like that, he thought, so concerned, so serious. Eyebrows angled slightly up towards the centre of his forehead! Michael drank in every detail of the boy's beautiful face. A face from one of those Greek vases in the British Museum.

"Thank you."

"Thank you, for what? I haven't done anything."

He would never know just how much he had done.

"Just thank you. Come on, let's be heading off, it'll be getting dark soon. We're only about half an hour from the shack. I think we both need some champagne."

It was almost six o'clock but still incredibly hot as they drove through Carlisle, past the tiny parade of eight shops and the two minute wooden churches, which stood oddly next to each other, St David's for the Anglican congregation, and The Sacred Heart for Catholic worshipers. The Carlisle Hotel, set back from the road on a large block of land, with not one solitary tree for shade, seemed oversized for what appeared to be such a small community. Next to it the garage, which doubled as a milk bar providing cooked chooks, hot chips, ice creams and cold soft drinks, for the town and surrounds. An empty block of land separated it from an imposing brick building, The Convent of The Sacred Heart, the last building in town.

Just a few hundred metres out of town, after a stretch of empty road bordered by gums, they rounded a bend and saw Riverlands.

"Home at last."

"That's not a shack!"

Riverlands looked magnificent, set at the end of long gravel drive; its two storeys surrounded by a wooden veranda and white painted iron lacework balcony

"No, not that," Michael laughed, "that's our posh neighbour's. Oh my goodness what a coincidence!" He flashed the boy a surprised look. Pulled up on the wide gravel drive in front of the grand white wooden house was the Toyota. The Donna Karan had been removed, but the dinner suit still hung in the back.

"Oh it's amazing, I just can't believe it, it's so cute," said the boy, excitedly as Michael turned on the light just inside the front door of the shack, revealing the living room in all its seventies glory.

When Michael had seen the tiny house for the first time, he had been totally infatuated in exactly the same way. It was like an exhibit from a museum. Seemingly nothing inside the house, except for an enormous television and a state-of-the-art fan on a shiny chrome stand, had been replaced or redecorated since it was modernised in the early 70's. And yet everything had been spotlessly clean and in mint condition, from the best tea set, with square saucers and a different coloured inside to each cup, to the patchwork bedspreads of crocheted wool squares. It was all so cosy, so evocative, like going to stay with invisible grandparents. They decided to leave everything just as it was, except the tv which they got rid of. They kept the fan.

"You won't ever change anything will you?" The boy's voice quietened and dropped, tailing off towards the end of the sentence, suddenly wary of perhaps treading too heavily on what was obviously hallowed ground.

Michael noticed, and understood. He was touched at the boy's obvious concern.

"Don't worry," he said, "It's cool. Help me open all the windows, it's so stuffy in here. There'll be loads of mossies, but I'll burn a couple of coils."

Michael switched on the fridge. The light came on and the motor seemed unusually loud. "You'll get used to the noise," Michael laughed, closing the door which had been wedged open with a matchbox, stuck to the door with Scotch tape. He turned to see the boy with his ruck sack over his shoulder.

"Where are we sleeping. Oh god, I mean... Oh, I'm sorry Michael. I just thought, well, I mean I thought that was what this was... I mean I thought that was the deal, I thought that was what you wanted, but..." The boy dropped his head blushing deeply.

Michael interrupted, his heart pounding.

"It is what I want. You don't know how much. It might surprise you, after the way I behaved earlier. But there's no deal. Of course I want to. But I just like being with you, so don't feel you have to, there are two bed rooms." It was Michael's turn to blush. They began to laugh at each other's embarrassment.

"So who do I have to shag around here to get a drink?" said the boy, lightening the atmosphere. They laughed, just a little too heartily.

"Well it's all in the eskies, but it's been so hot in the car, I hope it's still cold." Michael unzipped one of the plastic insulated cool bags. "God it's warm. We can't drink French champagne, warm. I'll whack it all in the freezer. It'll take at least an hour though. I've just switched it on. Why don't we just get some cold beers from the pub while we're waiting?"

"I've got a brill idea Michael. Presumably you're going to rustle up something delicious to eat, well there must be something in all those Tupperware containers, and frankly darl even after that huge burger at Anita's I'm ravenous. So, why don't you get on with the food, and I'll go to the pub and get some cold ones. And then, when we've eaten, you've got to show me everything," the boy giggled. "I mean, this place, the shack, and then perhaps you'd like to see my portfolio, my designs for the show."

Michael could hardly speak, he was so happy. It was all going so wonderfully.

"Perfect. You remember where it is, we passed it, it's not more than five minutes?" His eyes began to fill with tears again.

"I'm gone." The boy left immediately, tactfully ignoring Michael's obvious embarrassment.

The Butterfly Boy

Michael looked at his watch. Gone seven. Had the boy got lost? The table was set, everything was ready to go. All there was left to do was to dress the salad. Michael had to top up the water for the pasta twice as it boiled away.

Just as he was beginning to panic, the screen door swung to, with its distinctive metallic clang.

"I'm so sorry Michael. It was so hot, I just had to have a cold beer there and then, and then I got talking...!"

"I'm sure you did." Michael ruffled the boy's hair, and immediately couldn't quite believe he had done it. "Although who," the champagne cork popped, "you could have possibly found to talk to in the Carlisle Hotel, I can't possibly imagine."

" Oh I can always find someone to... Oh my god... you won't believe what I've done. I've actually left our beers in the pub... I'm so dizzy at times... I'll go back." The boy turned.

"No way, I'm not letting you out of my sight again, well not until we've eaten, I'm ravenous." The boy grinned sheepishly and Michael dared to ruffle his hair again. "Anyway, we don't need them now. The wine's cold, and I had a Scotch, well a couple actually. Sit down at the table, I've just got to dress the salad and put the pasta on. Do you want champagne or shall we save that for later? I've got some lovely Gewürztraminer, I'm so sick of Chardonnay!" He suddenly felt he was being pretentious, talking about wine like that, too serious, too mature.

"No, yes, whatever, it all sounds wonderful to me darl. Remember I'm just a poor student, but let's save the champagne for later, the night is young!" He flashed Michael a little look which sent shivers down his spine.

"These plates are gorgeous, were they in the house?" The plates were cream with a border shading from pale to mid apple green.

"Yes they're English, Art Deco, I saw some exactly the same in an antique shop in Katoomba, no, Mount Victoria, and they cost a fortune."

Dinner was perfect, Michael thought. He was pleased. He felt he had got it exactly right. The boy ate slowly and deliberately, obviously enjoying every mouthful.

"This wine is lovely. I've never tasted wine like this before. What did you say it was called?"

The boy emptied his plate but refused a second helping. Michael was surprised. At that age, he remembered, he could never eat enough. They had of course had the works at Anita's.

Michael cleared away the pasta plates and brought back the fruit.

"Shall I put some music on? Do you hate Lionel Ritchie?"

"No darl, anything as long as it's not Abba!"

Michael made a mental note to hide his Abba tapes if the boy ever came to his apartment in Sydney!

"Do you mind if I have some fruit later? Maybe for breakfast, I'm totally stuffed, and I'm dying to show you my drawings, although I'm a bit nervous, after all you did study fine art didn't you?"

Michael laughed. "Come on, we'll worry about the dishes later, champagne?" Michael came back from the tiny kitchen with the bottle and glasses, shallow bowl-shaped Edwardian crystal ones, not tall modern flutes. They too had been part of

The Butterfly Boy

the shack's treasure trove.

The boy was kneeling on the floor unzipping the large black portfolio. He then settled back between his bent legs, and sat with his bottom on the floor.

Michael opened the bottle carefully, poured two glasses, handed one to the boy, clinked it with his and said "Cheers."

"Cheers."

The boy looked into Michael's eyes, softly this time, affectionately? Michael dared to interpret.

He joined the boy on the floor, as close as he dare, his weight on one arm, legs stretched out on the other side. He put down his glass and opened the portfolio.

He slowly flicked over a page, then another, then back to the first page.

"They're beautiful, totally beautiful!"

Each page consisted of a large black cardboard mount, framing what appeared at first sight to be an abstract painting. Dark glowing colours, deep mossy greens, purples, velvety browns, the colours of jewels, of old stained glass, barely visible as if illuminated by the last rays of a setting sun. Then as Michael gazed at the page, a figure began to emerge. A face, with deep set glistening eyes, outstretched arms.

"They really are unbelievably beautiful images, but how could you ever translate them into reality, I mean?"

"Oh these are only the illustrations, the starting off point really. Each of these illustrations has a set of working drawings, really boring I'm afraid, but absolutely necessary, with all the seams and fastenings and measurements and back views. Anyway you'll see the finished products when you come to the show, won't you? You must hear the music I wanted, but can't have, I'm so upset but they're already using it for the opening scene."

The boy rummaged in his ruck sack, took out a tape and replaced Lionel Ritchie. "It's *Mezzanine*, the new Massive Attack album. Hang on, we want track four, 'Inertia Creeps'. It's totally fab."

"But how did you do them, the illustrations I mean?"

A husky whispering voice talked/sang in an erotic repetitive way to the frenzied sound of a throbbing drum rhythm and intermittent electronic sounds "Inertia creeps, moving up slowly,c'est chic, c'est chic."

"Ha, secret technique, but I don't mind sharing it with you darl. I know you won't steal it. It takes hours, coloured inks and wax resist, layer on layer, then lots more layers of varnish. That's what makes the colours iridescent, like butterflies wings!" He grinned cheekily.

Michael was surprised, confused, he had never confessed to the boy that he had given him the butterfly title.

For over an hour they both poured over and discussed the beautiful pictures. There were twelve, each similar, but subtly different. Michael was genuinely impressed, and the boy was clearly delighted by his reaction. Michael opened another bottle of champagne. The boy changed the tape.

"This is the music I'm actually having, 'Deep Forest Three', I suppose in a way it's better, more..... I don't know, more....what d'you think?"

"I think it's great, perfect." Michael poured more champagne. "God it's hot tonight isn't it?"

"Unbelievably. This river of yours, is it close? Can you swim in it?"

"Well yes, it's only a few minutes walk actually. It's not that deep at the moment, but yes, but well, I don't have any swimmers here."

The boy laughed. "Oh Michael you are funny, you can't be shy? Or are you worried about the neighbours. Anyway who's going to see us in the dark? Come on, I can't wait to cool down, it seems even hotter now than it was in the middle of the day." He jumped up pulling Michael up by the hand. "You must have some towels?"

The boy disappeared out of the door. The door made its hollow metallic clang. Michael grabbed two towels from a cupboard and followed him. The door clanged again. Should he lock up? Oh what the hell. Not like me to be so reckless, what's this boy doing to me? he thought.

At right angles to the road, a dirt track led down between two fences; one surrounding the long narrow garden of the shack, and opposite the sprawling manicured grounds of Riverlands. Behind the properties the track widened out bordered by two broad verges, once grass but now totally dry and then identical wire fences, electrified. In the light from the not quite full moon, they could see horses in the paddocks behind the fences, quite a few, pale with dark spots like Dalmatians.

"Appaloosas," explained Michael. "The Greens breed them. People come from all over the world to buy them."

After about five minutes walk the paddocks ended in what appeared to be a dark wall of tall trees. Michael pushed his way through a curtain of soft overhanging branches from a willow and scrambled down a dusty bank. The boy followed.

"Oh it's magic!" Before Michael could work out what was happening, the boy had ripped off all his clothes, dropped them in an untidy pile, sprinted across the pebbly banks of the river and disappeared into the dark water.

"Hurry up Michael, it's heaven."

Michael undressed, folding his clothes and laying them on top of each other in a small neat pile on the sawn off stump of what must have been a very large gum tree. Next to the pile of clothes he placed the two towels. He then took of his glasses, folded in the sides and placed them on top of the towels. He thought for a second, then moved them on to the pile of clothes instead.

The pebbles hurt his bare feet. How had the boy run with such agility without apparently getting hurt. Perhaps he really was enchanted?

The water was blissful as he sank in it to his shoulders. Not cold but decidedly cool, silky, and quite fast running. It seemed to mock him as it ran over his body, to entice him, pull him away from the boy. He let himself float down stream a little. It tickled him. He turned on his front and swam back. The boy was laughing loudly. Michael watched enthralled, as the boy repeatedly bent his knees, crouching, so that the water came to his chin, then jumped high into the air, twisting his naked body and arching backwards to dive back into the water. Shiny, dark, almost black. Agile, graceful, like a dolphin. Again and again he leapt and dived, laughing loudly each time.

Crazy boy, Michael thought. Crazy, crazy, adorable, beautiful, beautiful boy!

The Butterfly Boy

Michael suddenly remembered that they had drunk a bottle of wine and almost two bottles of champagne between them, and before that the boy had had how many beers in the pub! He waded closer to the boy, concerned. The water wasn't that deep, but there was quite a strong current. If any thing should happen? Oh god!

Close to, Michael could hardly bear to look at the boy, his body, each time it shot out of the water in a diamond shower of droplets. The moon also seemed to be in love with the boy, turning water into diamonds, caressing his dark glistening body, varnished by the river, like the boy's illustrations, exotic, mysterious, unbearably beautiful. Michael was mesmerised. He was also fascinated, that the willowy body was surprisingly muscular. He longed to touch it, to hold him, wet, gleaming, slithery, there in the river. He longed to hold him tight, to stop him jumping, to kiss him, to wrestle and play and splash him, and kiss him again. He ached with longing, was dizzy with desire, yet he couldn't pluck up enough courage to even take a step nearer. He merely stood, leaning forward against the current, intoxicated, enchanted, in love.

Then, suddenly, he was alone in the river, which seemed dark and slightly forbidding now, without the laughter, without the diamond display, without the boy, the dolphin, the butterfly.

Michael waded out of the river and across the pebbles, gingerly. He was glad of his foresight as he watched the boy discover the towels on the tree stump, snatch one up and begin vigorously rubbing his hair. He knew his rimless glasses were all but invisible in the dark. He was glad they were safe.

Michael joined him, suddenly very conscious of his nakedness, their nakedness. The boy seemed unbothered, but was suddenly, strangely quiet. Michael sensed a mood change. He shivered, then careful put on his glasses, dried himself and dressed. The boy was already dressed, and stood, back to Michael, slowly throwing pebbles into the river. Michael felt the heat of the night again.

"OK. Shall we go? We've still got the rest of the champagne to finish." He suddenly felt very nervous, panicky. What next? How would he ever make the move?

The boy slowly opened his hand, dropping the stone he was about to throw by his side. He turned slowly and walked towards Michael, silently. He stopped in front of Michael, close, still unspeaking. Michael's panic increased. Thunderous heartbeats. Embarrassed, he looked into the boy's face. It seemed expressionless. No clue! A second, maybe two, seemed like an eternity. Michael felt dizzy, he began to sweat.

Very slowly, deliberately, the boy raised his arms, one hand to either side of Michael's head. He paused momentarily, then gently, carefully removed Michael's glasses. Then, just as slowly, gently, deliberately, he leant forward until his lips brushed Michael's. Soft, brief, like a sudden warm little breeze, a kiss. Their first kiss.

Michael opened his eyes as the boy returned his glasses. Should he speak? What should he do? What was he supposed to do? Should he grab the boy, kiss him back, kiss him hard?

But the boy was gone, disappearing, dark, between the dark willows. Michael followed. He let the boy walk ahead, waiting for a clue. The boy stopped, and Michael, shadow-like stopped

The Butterfly Boy

too. The boy turned, and then he clearly saw the boy smile. Michael blessed the moonlight. The boy turned back and walked on.

Michael quickened his pace slightly so that within a few seconds he was walking alongside the boy. He turned sideways. The boy smiled again, a peaceful warm affectionate smile. Michael closed his eyes for a second and suppressed a sigh, a blissful sigh as the boy slipped his hand into his. They walked in silence, slowly, hand in hand.

As they passed Riverlands, it seemed there were lights on in every room . The car was gone.

Odd time of year for a ball, Michael mused. I wonder what the occasion is?

Michael removed his hand from the boy's, to open the gate. Another familiar metallic clink, not as grating as the screen door. He felt a sudden surge of happiness and extraordinary confidence. They walked either side of the car, which Michael had parked on the short gravel drive.

"What are you doing?" asked the boy as Michael opened the car door and reached inside.

"It's time to lay a ghost." He handed the boy the wet towels. "Here, hang these on the line, it's at the side of the house."

Michael carried the cassette into the house, unplugged the old portable radio, carried into the bedroom and plugged it into the wall by the bed. He slipped in the cassette, then rewound the tape to the beginning and as soon as he heard the metallic clunk, pressed the on button. The intro began, as the boy walked across the room and stood in the bedroom doorway.

"Michael? Are you really sure?"
"Come here."

Roberta Flack began to sing.
"The first time... ever I saw your face"

They stood a few feet from each other, eyes fixed in each others gaze, and undressed again. This time Michael like the boy, simply dropped his clothes on the floor where he stood.

*"I thought the sun, rose in the sky,
And the moon and the stars,
Were the gifts you gave!"*

They moved slowly closer, eyes, unblinking, locked together.

*"To the dark and the endless skies my love,
To the dark and the endless skies.
And the first time, ever I kissed your mouth,"*

Their second kiss, another gentle breeze, a sea breeze, salty from Michael's tears.

*"I felt the earth move in my hand,
Like the trembling heart of a captive bird,
That was there at my command my love,
That was there at my command, my love."*

They fell to the bed.

The Butterfly Boy

*"The first time, ever I lay with you
I felt your heart, so close to mine
and I knew our joy would fill the earth
and last till the end of time my love
And it would last till the end of time, my love."*

Michael held the boy's head in his hands and kissed his eyes, gently, repeatedly. Then his lips, again and again, and again.

*"The first time ever I saw your face,
Your face, your face, your face."*

Michael showered the boys face with soft, gentle breeze-like kisses. The song ended. Roberta's mood changed as she began a new song... The gentle breezes gave way to a mounting storm, their mouths exploded together, their bodies merged, outlines blurred, barriers gone, total intimacy. Roberta continued, unheard, to sing *"will you still love me tomorrow!"*

Unnoticed, unheard, unheeded, as the storm mounted.

🦋

Michael woke just before dawn. He simply could not stop smiling. He sat up and gazed at the sleeping boy in the half light, silently sleeping like a child. He lay on his stomach, head to one side resting on a bent arm. Michael resisted the urge to slip his arms around that adored body, a body now imprinted on his brain, his memory, his soul. He didn't want to risk wakening him.

Michael slipped out of bed and very quietly pulled on his clothes, which still lay in a crumpled heap on the floor. He looked at the other pile. He stooped and picked up the tee shirt in both hands. He squeezed it into a ball, pressing it to his face, silently kissing it. It fell to the floor, wet with fresh tears.

He very carefully closed the screen door behind him, using the handle to stop the spring from doing its job. For the first time no clang. He smiled to himself.

There was only one light showing through the glass panel of the front door of Riverlands as he passed. The car was in the drive. Michael wondered who had driven home. Had one of them decided not to drink? The boy? The girl? Had they had a good time? The perfect golden couple.

The horses were standing in groups near the gates in the fences. Waiting for their breakfast to be delivered? There was certainly not much for them to eat in the paddocks!

The light was dim and grey. The air was almost cool. Michael took a deep breath and then pushed his way, once more, through the now slightly damp curtain of willows. Now a magic curtain! How would it feel on the other side? Could he recapture the moment? Would he be able to 'see' it? He wanted to replay it and press 'save' to be sure he would never loose it. The memory must never fade.

At that moment, as if to prove the magic, the sun broke over the hill behind him, transforming the sleeping bush into a scene from a Disney cartoon.

Michael reached the tree stump. Perfect chair height.

Meditation was the one thing, apart from Mark, that had kept Michael sane over the last difficult years. He straightened his back and placed a hand face up on each knee. He tried to relax, to give in, to become more centred, to 'see' his breathing.

All he could see was the boy. Leaping and twisting. The diamond shower. After a while he managed to stop fighting the thoughts, the images, it only made them more persistent. As he let go, accepted the thoughts as mere thoughts, they came and went, became less frequent, and drifted away, until Michael was conscious of little more than a vague sensation of being filled with soft golden light. The noises of the bush were still there but faint, unimportant. The smells, the feeling of the warm sun on his back, the hardness of the tree trunk under his bottom. It all felt so right, so relevant, and at the same time totally unimportant. He let go more. He felt safe, part of it all, supported, looked after. He didn't have to do anything, just for now, he could simply 'be'.

His back began to feel very hot. He slowly opened his eyes and looked at his watch. He was surprised to find how long he had been there. He smiled and thought it would be alright to take the boy a cup of tea now. To waken him. And then... perhaps?

He stood up slowly, his legs slightly stiff after sitting in one position for so long. He walked along the track quite briskly, eager, impatient. When he reached the road, he stopped, surprised, bemused. Standing leaning against one of the white pillars of Riverlands' grand portico, the girl stood drinking a glass of what appeared to be orange juice. Hair loose but newly brushed. Bare feet. White pyjamas. But where was the car? It seemed odd. Perhaps she had driven it round the back into a garage? Hardly. Perhaps the boy, someone, had driven down the road to get milk, papers? It was still early, and only a few of minutes walk to the general store.

Michael let the door clang behind him this time. He stood rigid just inside. Something was wrong. He could sense it. What? The hairs on the back of his neck prickled. Hot as it already was, he shivered. What was it? He looked around at the debris of last night's meal. The glasses on the floor. The portfolio? Where was it? He felt sick. He put his hand on the door frame to support himself for a moment, then blinded by hot tears he rushed around the house. The bed was empty, the boy's clothes gone. The other bedroom? Empty. The shower? Tiles wet! Empty. He fell on the bed, sobbing violently. Something crackled under his chest. He sat up. A note!

He wiped his eyes with the back of his arm. He tried to focus on the words. His hand was shaking.

7.30 am
Michael

There was a message on my mobile when I woke up.
I've gone back to Sydney. I got a lift.

Sorry darling!

There was no signature, just a tiny drawing, a butterfly.

Michael felt sick. His head suddenly ached violently, like the worst migraine. He flung open the door and ran down the road to the gate of Riverlands. He stopped. Took a deep breath. Tried to calm himself. The garden seemed to be empty. "Oh god did that mean he would have to ring the bell?"

Then the golden girl appeared from around the side of the house, head down, still in pyjamas but carrying a large white rabbit. Michael opened the gate. The girl looked up.

"Hi."

She seemed very friendly.

"Excuse me, I know it sounds a bit nosey, but has your boyfriend driven back to Sydney this morning?"

"Brad? Brad's not my boyfriend, he's my brother." She laughed again, uproariously. "And anyway if he wasn't my brother he certainly wouldn't be my boyfriend, he doesn't like girls." She laughed again. "But, yes, he has just driven back to Sydney. He really is naughty, my grandparents are going to be furious, when they wake up and find him gone. We were supposed to be here for the weekend, but apparently he met some boy in that dreadful pub yesterday and he's gone back to Sydney with him. And I must say I'm not exactly thrilled about the prospect of going back on the train. Are you alright?" She put her hand on Michael's shoulder. "Oh god. What have I said? Oh no. The boy? Is there any thing I can do?"

" No, it's fine. I'm cool. Thanks anyway."

He turned to walk away, trying to appear calm, whilst all the time his head was bursting with pain, and wild racing jumbled thoughts... How could he? It all seemed so perfect. The boy seemed to have enjoyed it all just as much as he had. It seemed so perfect. It can't just have been for sex? It couldn't have been? Had he merely been another conquest? Part of a collection? Just a one night stand? No, no! Maybe there had been a message on the mobile? Maybe he had to go back for a fitting or something? Maybe this Brad was just being friendly giving him a lift. Fuck Brad. Fuck oh fuck the bastard. The perfect golden handsome fucking bastard. Maybe there was nothing in it? That fucking screen door!

Michael knew from experience with a headache as bad as this one that if he didn't manage to get to sleep as soon as possible, he would vomit. He threw himself on the bed. The note again.

The fucking note!

He dragged it from under his chest, screwed it into a ball and threw it angrily on the floor.

"Oh, why did David have to die? That fucking, fucking disease! It's certainly fucked up my life."

Michael looked at his watch. One thirty five. The bed was damp from his sweat. He could hardly believe how long he had slept. His head was surprisingly clear, but he felt numb, his body felt numb from having lain in the same position for all those hours. His mind felt simply numb, as if anaesthetised.

It all started to come back, but not in a rush, slowly, fuzzily, as if he was watching a video in slow motion. He felt strangely detached from the events of the past twenty four hours.

He sat up slowly, feeling oddly weightless, as if he wasn't really there. He didn't seem to belong to his surroundings. He felt like an observer, a ghost. Perhaps he was dead? People didn't die of headaches. Shock?

He felt terribly thirsty. He opened the fridge, took out a small bottle of beer, twisted off the cap and downed the contents in one go.

Ghosts can't drink beer. Michael laughed. How could he laugh, when he was feeling so awful? Not dead. Mad? He must get outside, some air!

He found himself walking back to the river. Was it a good idea? What the fuck, it couldn't get worse! He pushed his way through the willow and then immediately took a step back, making himself invisible again.

She was there, the girl, with a dog, throwing a stick into the river. Could he face it? Her? He would have to talk! Otherwise, the next easy place to get down to the river was quite a long walk. He would have to go back to the road. Oh what the fuck. She seemed nice enough. Maybe speaking to someone, only briefly though, would get rid of the mad feeling?

"Hi"

"Hi. Oh it's you. You OK?"

"Yea, cool. Bit of a hangover I think. Really, that's all, I'm cool."

She smiled, a funny little smile which showed a whole array of emotions in a split second. Concern, then slight disbelief, then simple, warm affection.

The dog, a red cattle dog bounded out of the water, dropped the stick at Michael's feet, then shook violently, soaking them both. It then gazed up in a pleading way straight into Michael's eyes. They laughed and the dog made a little noise, half way between a whine and a small woof, at the same time wagging the whole rear end of his body and pawing the stick.

"What a tart! He's worse than my bloody brother. Won't look at a mere female if there's a man around. In fact I think he's been indoctrinated by my brother. Perverted. Can you have gay dogs?"

They laughed again and Michael threw the stick as far as he could across the river. The dog launched itself into the river with an enormous splash, then started paddling furiously, chin up, towards the opposite bank.

"Look this is a bit embarrassing, and very cheeky in the circumstances, it being my brother who... well... the thing is, I'm kind of stranded, apart from the train, that is, and if you're driving back to Sydney today, I'd love a lift? But I quite understand..."

"Yes, of course," Michael interrupted. "It's not your fault. You can't be responsible for your brother. And to be honest, I'm feeling so shitty, I'm not too keen on driving all that way on my own. I'll happily trade a lift for a bit of company, so long as you keep the conversation away from your brother and my..... well, I just need distracting. Oh by the way I'm Michael."

"I'm afraid I'm called Rhyme! Yes, it's my maternal grandmother's fault. She insisted. She's very eccentric, and persuasive. You might have heard of her, she was a famous film star in the dim and distant past, Atlanta Ferrari."

"Really? You're joking! My god, of course I know her, who doesn't!"

"Well Atlanta Ferrari, born Molly Green, decided that my mother should land me with a corker of a name from the start. I ask you, Rhyme?"

"Well I think it's a fabulous name. Remember I'm just plain old Michael."

"You're hardly plain, Michael. Anyway, thanks, a lift will be great. What time do you want to set back? It's just that my other granny, the normal one, always does a proper tea at four thirty, and what with Brad having bolted, she'll be so upset if I don't stay. Would you like to come to tea? I mean we are neighbours, sort of."

"No, no. Oh I'm sorry I didn't mean to sound rude. Some other time, just not today. I'm not feeling exactly sociable. Just come round when you're ready. Any time. Whenever. I've nothing to rush back for."

Rhyme gave Michael a little pat on the shoulder and another funny little smile, sympathetic, reassuring, friendly.

Red, the dog, was wagging his tail and pawing the stick again. This time a real woof. Michael laughed and threw the stick once more.

"Well they say every cloud has a silver lining," said Rhyme, as Michael drew up in front of her apartment block in Rose Bay.

"If it hadn't been for my bloody tart of a brother, we wouldn't have become friends. We are friends aren't we Michael? God it's such a treat to have a proper sensitive conversation with a man who isn't just interested in trying to get inside your knickers."

"Of course we're friends." Michael ripped a bit off an empty envelope which he found in the glove compartment and wrote down his phone number. "I think I'm going to need a new friend. I simply can't dump any more on the friends I already have. I mean... Oh I'm sorry... I meant..."

"Do shut up Michael and stop apologising. You're beginning to get rather boring. Anyway that's what friends are for, and anyway we haven't even begun on *my* problems!"

A dull metallic silver envelope was pushed half under Michael's front door when he got back to his apartment at about eleven that night. 'Michael' was written in immaculate copperplate on the front in dark grey ink. He turned the envelope over. There was a blob of silver sealing wax holding down the triangular flap. A design had been pressed into the wax with a seal. A butterfly!

He ripped it open. No letter, no note, no message, just an invitation. Printed quite plainly in the style of a formal wedding invitation, but in silver ink on a rectangle of clear stiff plastic.

Michael crossed the landing and knocked on number four. Mark opened the door, wearing a white tee shirt and Calvin Klein underpants. He read Michael's thoughts.

"Oh, it's alright Michael. I'm on my own. I was just going to bed. Oh Michael it's all gone horribly wrong, hasn't it? I'm not going to say I told you so. Come in. You look like you need a large Scotch. As it's you I'll open my new bottle of single malt. God, you look a wreck. Oh it has gone wrong hasn't it my, dear friend? Did he rob you? Bash you? Come and sit down and tell your old mate Mark all about it."

"Well, I wasn't going to bother you, but this just arrived. It's on Tuesday. I just don't think I can go. But look Mark this isn't fair, you were just going to bed."

"Shut up, sit down, and drink this!"

It was almost 2 a.m. when Michael crossed the landing again and unlocked his own front door. He clutched the invitation, afraid it might disappear, dissolve, cease to exist. It was at least a way to see the boy again. He couldn't phone him. He wouldn't be able to cope. He knew he would just crack up if he heard his voice. Yes, that was the best way, in a crowd, he thought. He would be able to judge the situation. Know if he had a chance, or if it really had just been a one off.

The next day at lunch time Michael walked along Oxford Street looking for some new clothes to buy to wear for the fashion show. In Gowing's on Oxford Street he bought a pair of black Levi 501's. Very adventurous for him. He had only ever worn blue denim jeans. Then he jumped into a taxi to find a shop called Wilson Stuart further up the road in Paddington. Mark had suggested it. "Nice, interesting clothes, not too wild."

The two boys who were working in the shop couldn't have been nicer. He explained exactly what he wanted and showed them his new black jeans. The black cheese cloth shirt he tried on, they explained, was meant to be slim fitting, "body skimming". He wasn't so sure. It had taken him long enough to get used to baggy clothes. They didn't try and persuade him. But then he slowly began to get used to the 'new style' Michael who looked back at him from the long mirror at the back of the shop. He felt quite dashing, almost decadent, dressed all in black.

Walking back to work, he was less sure. He decided he would phone Rhyme and see if she would like to go out to dinner that evening. He would wear his new outfit and get her opinion.

She's going to say I look nice in it anyway, he realised. But it would keep him busy, spending an evening with his new friend. Keep his mind occupied for a few more of the interminable hours which separated him from seeing the butterfly boy again. He couldn't imagine what would happen. He wouldn't allow himself to think about it, to speculate. Even if he just caught a glimpse of the boy it would be better than nothing.

🦋

He arranged to meet Rhyme at the Gilligan's at seven. He was feeling quite bold, almost optimistic. He also thought that there might be a faint chance of bumping into the boy in the bar. Then he realised that it was highly unlikely, with the big show the next day. He felt sure that there would be all kinds of last minute finishing touches to be seen to.

Michael felt quite odd waiting for a girl. It felt almost naughty. All his friends were men, gay men. He was pleased that none of them were there. It was nice, he thought, to have a girl for a friend.

Rhyme looked stunning when she arrived, only a few minutes late, in cropped wide black linen pants and a tiny boxy white sleeveless top. On her feet she wore a pair of black cotton Chinese slippers, and on top of her head a pair of Oakley sunglasses held her hair back from her face.

"You look lovely. So chic."

"Why, thank you, kind sir. You can date me any time you like with compliments like that." She caught Michael looking at her ears.

"No, I don't wear any jewellery at all. Never. My extraordinary grandmother, Atlanta, the one that lumbered me with this silly name, claims women should never wear jewellery unless it's real. *And* very expensive. *And,* she insists, I'm too young for diamonds. If only! She's quite a character. You'd love her, actually, Michael. Unfortunately she never travels any more. She lives in Italy all the time now, in the grandest house, a palazzo really. She never even crosses the border to stay in her 'little' house in Provence, where she used to play *paysanne*. Anyway, Michael, I must say you're looking rather dashing yourself this evening."

Michael puffed up with pride, like a little boy in his first pair of proper long trousers.

Rhyme ordered a dry Martini, with an olive, and Michael ordered a beer. He didn't want to get too drunk. After their second drink, Rhyme suggested that it was time for some food and asked Michael if he minded going to a vegetarian restaurant.

"No not at all, I hardly ever eat meat anyway. Seafood yes, but..."

"Well you won't even get fish where I'm going to take you. It's completely vegan! I'm sure you'll love it though. It's called

Bodhi, in Chinatown, not very elegant, but wonderful food."

"It sounds really... Mark! What are *you* doing here?" Michael jumped up and gave Mark a big hug. "Mark, meet my new *girl* friend," he chuckled. "This is Rhyme. Isn't it a brilliant name? Rhyme this is Mark, my oldest friend."

"Best friend, please, Michael. I don't think we like the 'old' word do we?" They all laughed.

"Michael, if Mark's your best friend, why don't we persuade him to come and have a delicious Chinese veggie dinner with us? Make a little party of it. Oh Mark, that's very presumptuous of me, no doubt you already have a date?"

"No, I'm not meeting anyone in particular, just dropped in for a quick one. At a bit of a lose end, thought I might bump into one of the gang, Damian's usually in here. I certainly didn't expect to see you here Michael, and with a gorgeous girl friend. We are a bit of a dark horse these days aren't we Michael? Rhyme, I would love to join you both for dinner. If that's alright with you Michael." Michael gave him an affectionate little punch.

Rhyme laughed and got up from the table, dragging Michael up with one hand and taking hold of Mark's hand with the other, she pulled them off towards the door.

"Aren't I the lucky one with two dishy guys to escort me and no risk of being jumped on? Oh, Mark, I'm so sorry. I'm being presumptuous again, I just thought!"

"Don't worry Rhyme, it's totally cool." He slipped his arm around her waist as they turned from the staircase onto the still hot street. "I know I seem terribly butch, but I am also a friend of Dorothy!"

The Butterfly Boy

They all laughed uproariously and Rhyme, still laughing, hailed a taxi.

They continued to laugh over dinner as they played a game of speculating on the other diners in the dimly lit barn-like first floor restaurant. In turn they tried to guess who they were and what they did.

It was almost midnight when they dropped Rhyme off first in the taxi.

"Thanks for a lovely evening boys. I've really enjoyed myself. I hope we can do this a lot more. That's if you don't mind having a girl in the gang, and a PR at that! Who knows, I might convert you both, to vegetarianism that is!"

They all laughed one last time and then the taxi headed towards the bridge and the North Shore.

At first, Michael felt quite daring, quite avant garde in his new streamlined black outfit. Mark dropped round to give him a final once over just before he set off for the fashion show, and after giving him the thumbs up, had slipped back across the landing and returned immediately with a small parcel.

"A little present. A finishing touch, to bring you luck."

"Are you sure? I mean, I've never worn anything around my neck!"

Mark stood behind Michael and carefully knotted the fine leather thong. Michael walked over to the mirror, above the fireplace, to gauge the effect. It was very discreet, a small Buddha, carved from clear crystal.

"Thanks Mark. I love it. I really do. Well, I suppose if I'm actually going to go, I'd better be off."

Michael felt strangely invisible as he walked across the park to the huge circus tent, brilliant in alternating panels of electric blue and yellow. A large design was printed in metallic gold in each of the blue panels, representing the twelve signs of the zodiac. Twelve enormous flags billowed above the big top, proclaiming the name of the sponsor, Coca-Cola.

Around the main tent were several smaller white ones with open sides. Like medieval pavilions at a tournament, Michael thought. The growing crowds were being offered the choice of Coca-Cola in the traditional waisted bottles, or, Michael was amused to discover, miniature bottles of Krug champagne, also with straws! The atmosphere was heady. The noisy chattering crowd seemed almost over excited. The buzz of eager conversation was almost deafening. Michael scanned the gossips near by, anxious to discover a familiar face. If only Rhyme were there, he would feel so much more confident, more able to cope, he fretted.

He decided to centre himself by playing the 'who and what' game they had laughed so much over in the restaurant. Somehow it didn't work when you were on your own. He couldn't even begin to imagine who all these extraordinary people could be. Did they always dress like that? Why had he never seen these people before? Where were they normally, he wondered? There were so many of them. Michael felt at the

The Butterfly Boy

same time uneasy, yet fascinated by what his conservative teacher father would have instantly dismissed as 'a load of freaks.'

Michael studied a small group close by. A tall strongly built young man, had his complete face tattoo-ed in an elaborate, swirling almost lace-like design. Another was dressed entirely in white cotton, covered in burnt holes and scorch marks and had a design of swarming ants tattoo-ed up each arm.

The obvious leader of the curious group seemed to have the others spellbound as his voice whooped and squeaked in exaggerated falsetto tones. He was rather scary looking, yet somehow magnetically attractive. Dishevelled, and yet obviously, painstakingly studied in his disarray. Small, petite, his almost elf-like features were half hidden by a slash of scarlet make up, roughly smudged across the bridge of his nose. A crown of pale banana-yellow hair shot upwards in uneven floss-like points. Numerous studs, spikes and rings pierced several parts of his face and ears. His clothes, layer upon layer of them, in muted earth tones and rusty black looked as if they might have been buried in the earth for years. A garment which might have been described as a waistcoat appeared to be made from tree bark laced together with rough twine and was worn over a tight long-sleeved garment made from mesh, like a fishing net. The holes, however, were very uneven, and here and there odd small plastic toys, aliens, crucifixes and Indian deities, were tied into the mesh. Beneath, reaching almost to the ground, a rough, faded black, hand-woven rectangle of fabric, frayed at the edges, was wrapped around his narrow hips. This primitive sarong was secured with what appeared to be some kind of bone, speared through the layers of fabric.

One member of the little group, though hardly conservative, seemed to Michael rather out of place, although he couldn't work out quite why he felt this. His tangled curly shoulder-length hair, was bright orange-ey yellow. His skin was deep golden, his whole face, shoulders and bare arms, covered in tiny copper coloured freckles. He wore loose patchwork dungarees of patterned Indian fabrics and several pieces of ethnic silver jewellery. On the floor between bare freckled feet was a tribal-looking drum. Michael was particular fascinated by the hippie boy's eyes. They were green, large, bright and extraordinarily beautiful, yet somehow they seemed to be filled with an infinite sadness.

The mood of the little group suddenly changed. The boy with sad eyes looked at his watch and picked up his drum. He seemed rather agitated. The others calmed him with little pats and words of support. He handed his still half-full bottle of champagne to the boy in distressed white clothes, hurried off and disappeared around the back of the big top. The others downed their drinks and began to amble of in the same direction. The whole enormous crowd seemed suddenly to be on the move, pouring out of the white pavilions and heading towards the entrance of the giant blue and yellow circus tent. The buzz of voices, now fuelled by alcohol, was even more deafening as Michael was jostled inside. Everyone it seemed wanted to sit as near the front as possible. So did Michael. If only to possibly glance at the butterfly boy should he appear. But why would he? he thought. Surely he would be back stage, dressing his models? Oh god. Why have I come?

The Butterfly Boy

Inexplicably there was one single empty seat left in the front row, between a rather fierce looking older woman with scraped back hair and a large notebook, and a man with a greying pony tail and lots of cameras.

"Is this someone's seat?" Michael faltered.

"Are you from a magazine?" her voice boomed above the deafening crowd.

"No."

"Then it's free, darling." She picked up the programme, patted the empty seat and handed the programme to Michael as he sat down.

He turned to smile a thank you. She smiled back over half glasses.

"CHIC, darling."

Michael looked quizzical. She laughed.

"The magazine darling, not me, though my god I certainly try hard enough. Have to, darling, with all these young things snapping at my heels!"

Much to Michael's surprise all the lights suddenly went out. A murmur of shock ran like a wave through the crowd, and then after a few scuffling noises as the late-comers groped to find seats, silence. Michael suddenly noticed a smell. The strong smell of sawdust. He was surprised he hadn't noticed it before. It was as if the din of moments ago had suppressed his other senses. Then, in the dark and the silence, the faintest sound of muffled drumming. Incredibly faint yet close. A claw-like hand gripped Michael's wrist. A warm whiskey-tainted breath in his ear. A growled whisper.

"Darling, I do believe we have lift off. It can't be true. On time. On the bloody dot darling. This has got to be a first in the history of fashion shows! How novel! How divinely chic, darling!"

As the muffled drum beat gradually increased to a strong hypnotic tribal rhythm, a faint eerie light began to glow through a thick low-lying mist. Sitting cross-legged on the low circular barrier which enclosed the circus ring, the drummers began to materialise, faint silhouettes at first, they gradually began to take form. Twelve of them, sitting cross-legged, in an assortment of hippie rags.

As the drumming reached fever-pitch, a mass of laser beams suddenly shot upwards. All eyes followed to see a group of mirrored disco balls, clustered, in different sizes, high in the apex of the tent. Michael also noticed twelve empty trapezes, ranged in a circle high above the drummers.

Suddenly total silence, total blackness. Then in the dark a long low drum roll, and as the lasers once more hit the mirrored balls, filling the tent with countless brilliant moving stars, the curtains at the back of the arena slowly opened and out billowed clouds of dense mist. The drums resumed their sensuous jungle rhythm and an enormous colourful figure appeared through the white clouds. Over three metres tall, it wore a towering top hat, tail coat and long skinny trousers covering obviously stilted legs. A giant whip-wielding ringmaster clattered slowly into the centre of the tent. A scarlet sneer was painted onto a dead white face. His eyes flared in a sinister way as his red leather whip flashed and cracked around the ring.

The talon gripped Michael's arm again.

"Darling how clever! Look the whole thing's made from

opened out Coca-Cola cans, like armour. These young things are just too clever."

Three more giants gradually appeared and circled slowly, clattering in their jointed metallic costumes. One with an enormous skirt, reaching out a metre either side like an Eighteenth century court costume. Another in exaggerated mediaeval dress with a tall pointed headress. The third seemed based on Elizabeth the first, with a neck ruff as large as a cart wheel. As they began to clatter their way slowly towards the curtains, to disappear once more into the mist, Michael became aware of a new movement. Unnoticed, the twelve trapezes had been lowered, and, the twelve drummers, still drumming, were being hoisted to the top of the tent. The crowd began to murmur in approval, but before the noise grew louder than a faint hum, it was drowned by a blast of ear-splitting techno music, as a group of models in brilliant rainbow coloured outfits, burst dancing into the ring. The first collection of clothes.

For over an hour Michael's senses were bombarded. He had never experienced anything like it. Some collections were less outlandish than others, but all seemed extraordinarily original and witty and no two were even slightly similar.

Towards the end of the show, to the accompaniment of a solitary digeridoo, a huge inflatable model of Ayers Rock grew out of a suitcase, which appeared after a brief blackout. This penultimate collection, modelled against the spectacular backdrop, was a group of hand painted swim and resort wear entitled Bush Babes, Michael noticed in his programme. The brilliantly hand-painted fabrics representing Australian native flora and fauna, were quite dazzling.

Michael's heart sank. Surely however good the butterfly boy's clothes were going to be, they could never eclipse this sensational collection.

The applause was deafening as the models pranced off and Ayers Rock gradually sank back to the ground.

Once more a whisky-laden purr. "Daarling, *entre nous*, I've heard on the grape vine that this next boy's tipped for the top. Rising star, darling!" Her eyes widened and she gave Michael a confidential little nod as she opened her handbag and took out a Louis Vuiton silver flask. She flipped open the lid with a little twist and offered it to Michael, who politely shook his head. She threw back her head and drank deeply.

"Well that's a tad better at least, but I'll tell you what though, daarling, I'm simply dying for a fucking cigarette... Oh and darling, they say he's totally divine looking!" She gave Michael a knowing look over the top of her whiskey flask. "Oh, eyes forward, we're off again darling." Total black out.

Once more twelve shadowy figures began to emerge, dimly, very faint, through a swirling mist. But this time to total silence. They stood frozen, arms stretched out straight, at shoulder height. As Michael's eyes adjusted to the gloom, he realised that they were completely naked. He also realised that the naked model closest to him was familiar. He was sure he recognised her from somewhere, the blonde crew-cut, the Celtic tattoos. He remembered.

Her pubic hair, as blonde as the hair on her head, was cut short, and trimmed into a small perfect triangle. A larger triangle of fine silver chain connected the rings in her nipples and navel.

The Butterfly Boy

"What a divine creature, darling," The whiskey breath almost made Michael choke. "God she's making me dribble." A rough cough turned into a quiet but decidedly obscene laugh. Michael shuddered.

The music started. It was Massive Attack, track four 'Inertia Creeps', Michael realised. He smiled. Somehow the boy had got his own way. Of course, there had just been the drums at the beginning of the show!

Lasers shot upwards once more, but this time from the floor in the centre of the ring. All eyes darted upwards. Hanging bat-like, from the trapezes, were twelve blonde tanned muscular boys, naked except for tiny sparkling gold jock straps. Each held something which seemed like dark multicoloured twisted rope, stretched tightly from hand to hand.

The trapezes descended slowly until, suspended just above the naked models, the blonde Adonis's flicked their hands, unfurling the ropes which then dropped over the girls. Gossamer webs of dark glowing colours. Twelve shimmering butterflies. The audience seemed to take in a deep audible breath in unison.

The golden boys were slowly hoisted back up again and the butterflies began to shudder slightly. Then, one by one, they each gave a tiny jump on to the points of their toes. Michael noticed that they were wearing flesh-coloured ballet shoes. Gradually they began to move their 'wings', then one by one they began to descend from their positions on the raised circular barrier. Still on points, they lowered themselves gingerly into the ring. With fast tiny jabbing movements, they constantly moved their weight from toe to toe. Their bodies and wings, by contrast, gracefully rocking and swaying in slow motion. Gradually a vast column of light, about four metres across, appeared in the centre of the ring, blazing upwards onto the mirrored balls and bouncing back as dazzling points of light into the spellbound audience. The butterflies, seemingly mesmerised by the light, began to move towards it, occasionally jerking a pointed toe high up to their knees, as if it were suddenly burnt.

The music grew louder and louder, as the dancers nervously picked their way through the invisible obstacles, towards what seemed to be the brilliant central sanctuary. As each dancer entered the column of light, the extraordinary beauty of their costumes became immediately apparent. The colours blazing gloriously, the embroideries flashed and sparkled. The dancers began to swirl and intertwine, forming one writhing, shimmering iridescent living sculpture. One by one photographers rushed forward from the audience, flashing and clicking in a frenzy. The volume of the music grew to almost ear-splitting proportions, and the audience began to rise to their feet clapping louder and louder. As if triggered by the increased volume of noise, the trapeze artists began to swing backwards and forwards in perfect unison, higher and higher, and then on the very last note of the music, their hands met and held, forming a perfect circle of glorious tanned bodies, like a golden capitol, crowning the top of the pillar of light. At the same moment the butterflies froze. The audience froze. The cameras stopped flashing, and after what can only have been a couple of seconds, the tent was once more plunged into total darkness.

Michael was aware of an intense pain in his arm as the

talons dug deep. Then, the grip was released as the audience, once more burst into wild applause, shouting "Designer, designer."

The lights suddenly blazed. The mirror balls once more splattered the rapturous audience with brilliant shooting stars. The ring was totally empty. As were the trapezes. The roar grew louder and louder, until at last the curtains parted, and there alone, dressed in simple black tee shirt and trousers, stood the butterfly boy.

Michael thought he was going to faint. As the audience applauded louder and louder, the boy walked calmly and confidently to the centre of the ring, where he dropped his head modestly, then bowed low from the waist. He then stood upright, turned slowly, and with both hands gestured towards the open curtains, as a conductor might invite an audience to show their appreciation of his orchestra. A moment's pause, then suddenly the boy was surrounded by a frenzied crowd of designers, dancers, models, drummers and trapeze artists, jumping and waving, dancing and drumming. The boy was totally obscured from sight. Michael's whisky-breathed neighbour was scrabbling her way, notebook in hand to the front of the scrum, as the audience poured over the barrier into the ring. For a split second Michael caught a glimpse of the boy, beaming with pleasure, chattering. Behind him was a familiar face. The golden boy, Brad, Rhyme's brother. Michael wasn't really surprised, but suddenly his whole body felt like lead. Intense excitement instantly turned to intense depression.

What was the point? How could he ever compete? Why had he ever come? He rose and turned to push his way against the tide of bodies fighting towards the centre of the tent. Once more his eyes were blinded by hot tears. He was glad to know that Rhyme wasn't there, or any of his friends, to witness his pathetic state.

Fighting his way to the exit, he didn't see the boy waving furiously at him.

🦋

The park appeared totally empty, as he headed towards the city. He was glad. He needed to be totally alone, to walk, to try and pull himself together.

A dog appeared out of the darkness. Michael stopped. A sympathetic, non-judgmental friend? The dog sniffed at Michael's legs, momentarily, in a disinterested way, then disappeared in the direction of the circus tent.

🦋

Michael was surprised to see the size of the crowd spilling out onto the pavement outside the pub. The Albury was normally only that busy at he weekends. Then he remembered their had been an awards ceremony, for Mardi Gras, in the Town Hall that evening. That's where everyone was from, finishing off the evening.

The twenty minute walk had calmed him somewhat, the tears had stopped. Perhaps the raucous crowd would distract him? The loud overtly gay vulgarity might anaesthetise the pain a little.

The Butterfly Boy

A transvestite was performing on top of the bar, miming to a Whitney Houston song. As two muscular arms in shoulder-length red PVC gloves shot upwards, heralding the end of the number, two implanted breasts were forced together. Michael felt faintly nauseous as one small pink nipple appeared above the edge of the scarlet sequinned neckline.

There was a small commotion as a group of drunk, and obviously straight young men, who turned out to be American sailors, stumbled into the bar, holding each other up and laughing uproariously. They began pointing at the drag queen, who stood high above them on the bar, her stilettoed feet wide apart and her large gloved hands on narrow red sequinned hips. A fuschia sneer, carefully outlined in deeper pink, foretold mischief to come. And indeed it wasn't long before one of the poor unsuspecting lads was up on the bar being humiliated. Within seconds his less than average sized penis had been exposed, and was being fingered and ridiculed in front of all his straight mates, and a crowded pub full of gay men!

"You're not laughing, darling, why so sad? Someone as gorgeous as you shouldn't be alone and sad. Come and join our little party," a low voice purred into Michael's ear, and a small smooth and surprisingly cool hand slipped into his and began to pull him away from the bar.

How strange! What a coincidence! thought Michael. Except that Sydney *is* so small. It was the leader of the little group of gossips from earlier in the evening. The voice however, now no longer rising and falling in exaggerated falsetto notes, but low and seductive. Michael was intrigued the boy hadn't stayed with the crowds at the circus tent. They must have got a cab?

he speculated.

The boy, who was surprisingly strong, dragged Michael to the back of the pub, dark eyes flashing and cajoling.

"Come on beautiful man, join our little party. We'll look after you. We'll make you happy again. Come away from those boring straight people." Michael couldn't understand why the boy would be interested in someone like him.

The odd little group which had fascinated Michael in the tented pavilion were reassembled again around a small chest-height black table, cluttered with glasses and shining with spilt alcohol. Stuck to the centre of the table, in a pool of it's own wax, was a single black candle.

"See, darling, much more fun at our little party, have another drink darling. Jay, get our gorgeous new friend a proper drink. Not a boring beer!" The tall boy in the burnt white clothes and ant tattoos, grinned and moved towards the bar.

"But..!" Michael fumbled in his pocket.

"Don't be dull, darling. You're far too gorgeous to be boring! This is *our* little party. You're our guest. Our new little friend. Our gorgeous, gorgeous little toy. Our new little plaything." The boy shrilled, rat-like, but somehow enticing, oddly attractive.

Over what seemed like a very short period of time Michael got very drunk, as the hypnotic rat-like boy regaled him, and the boy's obviously adoring acolytes, with extraordinary stories of ritual orgies. All the time he clung erotically to Michael, gently stroking his neck, running strong slim fingers up and down his spine and through his hair.

At some stage, Michael couldn't quite remember when, the

The Butterfly Boy

hippie drummer boy, still in patchwork dungarees, had joined the party. Silent, he smiled weakly at the rat boy's stories, but whenever he raised his eyes from their habitual lowered position, staring at his own hand wrapped around a glass, they met Michael's.

Such soft eyes, strange, questioning, pleading? Another lost soul? Another guest at this insane party? Another gorgeous little toy? Michael wondered.

The stories became more and more bizarre. At one point, the rat boy, without interrupting his tale, turned sideways and removed a packet of cigarettes from the hand of a surprised man, who stood close by watching, the latest act on the bar. The boy put a cigarette in his mouth and another behind his ear.

"Light!" he demanded of the stranger, who meekly complied.

"Michael, if only we'd known you a week ago, I could have got you an invite to Dina's crucifixion party. It was deeevine!"

"Excuse me." Michael stumbled in the direction of the gents.

The smell of urine was overwhelming. He decided to try and escape. To get away from the party. Suddenly he couldn't cope. Where was it all leading? Not his scene. What did being a 'gorgeous new toy' involve? Crucifixion parties? Was it a joke? Oh, god! His thoughts began to race.

"You OK? Trying to escape too? Come on, this way. He's actually very sweet you know, very clever, when he's not out of his head." Michael was surprised at the English accent and suddenly realised it was the first time he had actually heard the drummer boy speak. Once again a hand slipped into Michael's, but this time larger, warmer, firmer.

"I don't suppose... that... you'd like to... come back to my place?" the boy asked, shyly, falteringly.

He looks beautiful, Michael thought. Soft, appreciative, gentle. His tousled hair, with the light behind it, golden, like a young prince's in children's fairy story.

"Yes, I would," Michael was surprised to hear himself reply.

In the short taxi ride to King's Cross, they exchanged names. Fred, the drummer boy told Michael that he was twenty seven, although he knew he looked much younger, and normally worked as a chef aboard cruise liners. Drumming was only a hobby.

"Where did you train to be a chef? In England?"

"In the army."

"The army?"

"Yes, I know, I don't exactly look the type to have been in the army. You'd be surprised how different I look at work, with my hair tied back and conventional clothes."

"But why the army?"

"Perhaps I'll tell you later... We're here." He jumped out and paid the Chinese driver through the window.

"No lift, I'm afraid. Grotty building, but really cool flat... It's not mine. It's Gary's. He's a friend of mine. Qantas steward. He's hardly ever here. He let's me use it whenever I'm in Sydney, and he uses my flat in London. It's a perfect deal."

The Butterfly Boy

The apartment was immaculate. It could only belong to a gay man, Michael thought. It looked exactly like a feature from *Wallpaper* magazine. Michael sat on a caramel coloured leather settee, long and perfectly plain, no arms, dark tapered wooden legs.

"I'm going to shower. Champagne? Well not real. It's Ozzie. But it's quite nice. I mean, oh I'm sorry, I seem to spend my life apologising."

Michael sipped his drink and studied the room. Beige walls, pale wooden floor, the latest magazines ranged impeccably on the over-sized glass coffee table. A deep-pile cream wool rug in front of the empty fireplace, which had been totally covered in mirror. He turned to look behind him at the three large framed black and white Herb Ritts photographs.

Oh god! Should he try and get out of it? Michael tortured himself. No, the boy wouldn't understand. He'd be hurt. He seemed like such a nice kid. Well not exactly a kid, but?

Fred stood in the doorway, looking even more like a fairy tale prince. A little boy even? Wrapped in a huge white towelling bath robe. His wet hair, now dark, the colour of tarnished copper, stuck to his neck like snakes.

"Would you like a shower? Oh no! I didn't mean..."

"Yes. I'd love one."

"There I go apologising again. Sorry. Out of the door, second on the left. The loo's the first door, and the bedroom's opposite. Look are you sure? I mean," Fred hung his head and laughed.

"I'll take the bottle into the bedroom. Here have a top up for the shower. I've put a clean towel out for you, and a ... new toothbrush, if you want it that is. No, I'm not going to apologise. It's bedtime. Everyone cleans their teeth at bedtime don't they?" He laughed again, but somehow it didn't seem quite natural. Michael showered quickly.

The bedroom was totally white, immaculate with a white painted floor and no decorative features whatsoever. The champagne bottle and the half-empty glass seemed like a vulgar intrusion.

Michael who had been having serious second thoughts as the shower sobered him up somewhat, had an instant change of heart when he saw Fred, lying there, golden and naked, the only feature, except for the bottle and glass, on a perfect empty white canvas looked sublime. A golden god, stretched out on tight white cotton. Still-wet hair, staining the pillow with damp.

The young god's body - Icarus? - was freckled and tanned all over, no white swimming trunk marks. Lean and muscular, like a gymnast, totally shaved. His circumcised penis lay, half-erect, diagonally across a perfect flat golden stomach.

Michael climbed silently onto the bed. He kissed Fred's forehead, softly, oh so gently. Michael was feeling more aroused than he could remember for a long time, masterful, aggressive almost, yet he sensed that this was a time to hold back, to be gentle. To slowly awaken the sleeping prince, to gradually arouse this dazed golden god, fallen from the heavens.

He kissed the chin, then gently but swiftly, like a pecking bird, he kissed up the left hand side of the boy's passive face, across his forehead and down the other cheek back to the chin. He backed away, supporting himself on outstretched arms to gauge the effect of this new spontaneous experiment in foreplay.

The boy opened his eyes, smiling eyes, yet still strangely sad.

"That's so sweet. No-one's ever done that to me before. A ring of kisses. What a nice present. Thank you." He closed his eyes and let out an almost inaudible sigh.

Michael planted one feather-like kiss on each closed eyelid.

He arched back again to drink in the beautiful face. His garden of new kisses. Would they blossom? he speculated. A flicker of a smile seemed to pass over the mouth, ever so slightly open. A smile? Michael mused. Mouths show nothing. Only eyes tell the truth. And yet?

The lips responded to Michael's, but slowly, faintly, haltingly. Michael felt a hand on the back of his head. A touch so slight, so wary, as a mother might caress the forehead of a feverish child.

Michael's mouth, his gentle worshipping kisses, worked down the taught slender neck, then backwards and forwards, across and down, flat lean muscles, smooth concave armpits. Then arms, hands, fingers. At last an imperfection, fingernails bitten almost into non-existence. Each received a kiss.

But suddenly, almost violently the hand was dragged away from Michael's adoring mouth. In a split second the boy had spun his body face down, arms outstretched, hands wedged firmly under his thighs, head on one side turned away from Michael. His perfect golden athlete's shoulders jerked in unison with the muffled heartrending sobs.

"I'm sorry." Barely audible.

"It doesn't matter. Honestly. Please!"

Michael, gently, gingerly put a hand on each shoulder, and as if he had touched some unseen trigger, the boy spun around once more, his arms tight around Michael's neck, his wet sobbing face pressed hard into Michael's chest.

"P... pl... please, hold me, I'm so sorry, please, hold me."

Eventually, after what seemed an incredibly long time, the sobbing began to subside. Michael realised that he hadn't thought about his own sadness for quite a while. It made him feel strangely better, stronger, to be able to comfort someone else. Sad beautiful boy! He patted his shoulder, barely perceptibly, as the crying eventually grew less and less.

Suddenly the boy sat up, with his back to Michael, knees pulled up to his chin, arms wrapped tightly round his knees.

"Michael?" he asked in a surprisingly calm tone.

"Yes?"

"Can I ask you something?"

"Of course."

"Please will you stay for a while? I'm sorry, I don't think I can... well you know... well not at the moment, but, well, I'm just feeling incredibly low, I would just give anything not to be on my own at the moment."

He spun round again to face Michael. Michael had never seen such pleading, such desperation, such intense sadness.

"Try and get rid of me." Michael attempted a little laugh.

The boy's eyes were locked onto Michael's, unchanging.

"Thank you. You don't know how grateful I am. Shall I make us some tea? Herbal?"

The Butterfly Boy

"I'd love some. I'll get up for a bit. I need a pee."

Michael put on another towelling dressing gown which he found hanging behind the bathroom door, and went back into the sitting room. The light was still on. He sat on the settee again.

"Thank you, Michael." The sad eyes attempted a smile. He handed Michael a glass and chrome mug. The steaming golden liquid was strongly perfumed by the floating twigs and berries as Michael touched the too-hot glass to his lips.

Fred put his drink on the glass coffee table and sank to the floor, still naked, he slowly lowered his head onto Michael's knee and put his arms around his waist.

"That OK?"

"Of course." Michael leant awkwardly forward and gently kissed the top of his head.

"Michael?"

"Yes?"

"Have you got a Mum and Dad?"

Then began a story of such heartrending sadness, Michael could hardly believe it was true, except he knew that it was. Fred's mother, a prostitute, had walked out of the hospital in the north of England two days after he was born. He had only discovered this quite recently, when he had been allowed access to the records of the home where he was brought up. It had been closed down after abuse exposures.

"Were you?"

"Yes. From the age of about six."

"Oh god!"

"See this scar?"

Michael couldn't believe he hadn't noticed a long livid scar down the outside of Fred's left thigh.

"Cancer! From the age of eleven, I was in hospital for three years. Then back in the home. All the other kids were on drugs. I never did drugs. Not once. I saw what happened to them. I knew that staying clean was the only way to survive. The only way out! I joined the Territorial Army when I was fourteen. I needed role models. I knew I had to learn self-discipline if I was to survive."

"It helped?"

"Yes, and as soon as I was old enough to get out of the home I joined the army. I loved it actually. It was real. It was hard, but at least I wasn't being lied to any more, or abused. Do you see your parents often?" The arms tightened around Michael's waist. He knew Fred was crying again.

"Yes, well, quite often. They live in Melbourne. Well outside. Dad's a bit conservative, a bit old fashioned, but mum, well she's lovely."

The head dug in harder, arms vice-like around Michael's waist.

"Come on, sad beautiful boy. I don't think all the love in the world could heal your wounds. Come on, allow me to love you, just for tonight, come on." He dried the boy's eyes on the sleeve of the bath robe, dabbing them gently. Then he took his hand and led him back to the bedroom, turning off the lights as they passed the switches by the door.

Next morning Michael was awakened by the smells of coffee and bacon.

"Come on, breakfast's ready. You can shower later."

"Good job Rhyme can't see me eating bacon."

"Rhyme?" The boy seemed perfectly normal, bright, cheerful almost!

"Yes. Funny name isn't it. She's a new friend of mine. She's trying to turn me into a fully signed up veggie!"

"Oh Michael, I never thought to ask. I'm sorry. I'll do you some mushrooms instead."

"Don't you dare take it away."

"Michael?"

"Yes?"

"Just, thank you."

"I wish I could really help, make it all go away for you."

"You can't. No one can. Most of the time I can keep a lid on it. Keep the nightmares at bay. But, just sometimes!"

There was one message on his answer machine when Michael got home from work the next day. Even though it was not yet eight in the morning, Michael opened the freezer put some ice cubes in a glass and poured himself a large Scotch. He listened to the message three more times.

"Michael, you beast. What happened to you? Did you hate it? I know you were there. I saw you, right in the front row, with Marion Russell-Clyde of all people. Was she as scary as they say? Is she really an old dyke? Do phone me. You're not angry with me are you? I'd love to see you. I'm not so frantically busy now. *Do* phone!"

He poured himself another drink and picked up the phone.

At exactly seven that evening, the doorbell rang. He stood there, grinning, holding out a single, rather battered looking rose.

"I won't ask where you got it." Michael pulled the boy inside, took the rose from his hand, threw it on the floor, took the boy's head in his hands and kissed him very hard on the mouth.

"Gosh Michael!" the boy gasped for breath.

"I intend to make hay while the sun shines." He kissed him again.

"Hungry?" Michael was surprised at his own behaviour, his words? Where had this new sudden confidence come from? he wondered.

"Thai? Japanese? Chinese? Have you ever been to Café Cairo?

"Oh I love Thai, and I'm ravenous."

Over dinner they talked mostly about the fashion show. The boy's premature disappearance from the shack was never mentioned. Neither was Michael's from the show. And, although Michael did regale the boy with what he thought was an amusing description of the scene in the pub, the drag queen, sailors, freaks party etc, he didn't mention Fred, and although he knew that he would have to broach the subject of his new friendship with Rhyme at some stage, for the time being he avoided the issue.

The Butterfly Boy

Next morning Michael was awakened by the boy's mouth, hot and hungry, expertly exploring his body. For a while he simply lay there, eyes closed, passive, luxuriating in blissful anticipation, waiting to discover where the butterfly would land next! There was no logic, no natural progression, all of which made the delicious torture all the more exciting.

Suddenly, as if an elastic band had been wound to its limit, Michael jumped up, and laughing, threw the boy onto his stomach, hand tight round the back of the boy's neck he pinned him to the bed, suddenly, newly strong, masterful, aggressive.

Afterwards, the boy lay on his back, panting. For the first time, Michael noticed, he was actually sweating, not heavily, but his slight body glistened with a faint sheen of moisture.

"Shit Michael, you certainly know how to fuck a boy, so that he stays fucked!"

Michael inwardly glowed with pride at the compliment.

"Oh god, is that the time. I've got to go. I've got an interview with *Vogue* in less than an hour and it's bloody miles!"

Michael lunged at the boy, arms tight round his waist, head crushed onto his slender smooth chest.

Oh god it was all going wrong. Why was he crying? He wondered. Stop! Don't spoil it! Oh fuck, don't speak! Too late!

"Don't go! Please don't go!"

The boy gently prized Michael's arms from around his waist, pushing him away as tactfully as possible.

"But I've got an interview with *Vogue*. *Vogue* Michael!... I think we need to talk."

"OK." Michael tried to stifle a sob.

"Can you meet me at lunch time?"

"Yes. What time? Where?"

"God where?- Do you know the Chinese Gardens. Darling Harbour. Do you know it? There's a tea room. Quarter past one?"

"Yes... but, please, please, just at least let me get you some coffee, tea, juice, whatever?"

"Thanks Michael, but no, I must go. A quick shower though? A towel?"

Michael was five minutes late, and in a state of panic. Two volunteers had phoned in sick, so he had had to man one of the helplines. The last call had been a tricky one. He hadn't been able to cut it short. He ran through the gardens, not noticing how beautiful they were, along bamboo-lined walkways, through shady pavilions with round entrances. A plump fair haired girl stood by the lake, decked out in traditional Chinese costume, having her picture taken by a professional photographer. He didn't even notice how ridiculous she looked.

He did however notice the smell of the place. The hot air was heavy with the almost sickly fragrance of gardenias. He reached the stone steps which led up to the tea room and stopped to take a breath, to centre himself. He took a Kleenex from his jeans pocket and wiped his face, then removed his glasses and wiped them. Then, consciously forcing his breathing to slow down, to become deeper, he nervously climbed the stairs.

The Butterfly Boy

The interior of the tea room was lovely. He had never been there before. The dark wooden room was bathed in blue light from the beautiful stained glass windows, decorated with simple pictures. There was an all pervading feeling of peace and calm. Although Michael could sense the atmosphere of calm, he couldn't make himself be a part of it. His body had recovered from its physical exertion, but his heart was still racing, his stomach churning. Butterflies! he thought.

There was only one table occupied, by two smartly dressed middle-aged women, heads close together over the low table, involved in an intense and obviously serious conversation. They didn't look up. On the far side of the room, doors opened onto a balcony, which overlooked the lake. The boy sat in profile, obviously unaware of Michael's presence. He appeared like a dark silhouette against the brilliant light of the gardens. Dressed in black, he seemed to be staring straight ahead, into space, oblivious of the group of sparrows, inches from him fighting for crumbs off the table. One hand rested around a small Chinese tea cup, the other moved slowly backwards and forwards in front of his face, holding a scarlet paper fan.

He turned as Michael approached, giving him an odd little half-hearted smile.

"Crazy isn't it?" He flicked the fan shut and dropped it on the table, scattering the sparrows. "I bought it from the shop at the entrance. It was only three dollars. Oh, I'm sorry. I forget to tell you that you have to pay to come in. It's just that I love it here. I thought we would be relatively alone."

Michael sat down opposite the boy, who despite the frivolity of the paper fan, seemed in a very serious mood. He stretched out and gave Michael's hand a little squeeze, as a young waitress approached.

"Would you like to see the menu sir?"

"Er... no. No thanks, I'll just have a drink. What are you drinking?"

"Jasmine tea."

"That'd be fine. Thanks."

The sparrows had reassembled on the wooden balcony, right next to their table. An unnoticed audience.

"Look this is... I mean... Oh god... I mean, look, I'm sorry... Can we?"

"Michael. Please, let me talk first. This is really difficult. I don't know quite how to say it, but, look, I really like you. I mean I really, really like you, a lot. I love being with you. I love talking to you. I love having sex with you. But Michael I'm just not ready for a full on relationship. Darling, I'm too young to settle down. Life's a box of toys. I want to go out and play. To be honest, I can't imagine I'll ever be a one man guy. I'm just a little tart really. I'd only hurt you. I'd hate that. You're too nice. I like you too much. Maybe in a few years?"

The girl brought Michael's tea.

"Thank you."

"Look, I'm not saying we shouldn't see each other. I want to. I'd love to. We could still be fuck buddies. And do other things, movies, restaurants, sometimes. It's just I'm worried you'll get too serious. I know that sounds conceited, and I've probably got it all totally wrong and am making an absolute fool of myself."

The Butterfly Boy

Michael sat there trying to hold back the tears. He couldn't speak. He daren't speak. The boy squeezed his hand again.

"Drink your tea."

Michael shook his head. The boy passed him a paper napkin. Michael removed his glasses, wiped his eyes, blew his nose. The boy took the glasses out of his hand, cleaned them on his black tee shirt and handed them back. Michael managed a little smile.

"Don't talk Michael. Think it over. I really do want to keep on seeing you, but you decide. I'll do whatever you want to do, and if you think it's best we don't see each other at all, well perhaps for a while. That's cool. Why don't we have a little walk in the gardens? We've paid, haven't we. Have you got time? What time do you have to be back at work?"

"Yes. Let's. I'm fine for a while. Well, I can't be that late back. I'll just go to the boy's room."

Michael splashed his face with cold water and tried to pull himself together. He tried to make himself think logically but his mind seemed strange, dull. He couldn't seem to make it work normally. He looked in the mirror. He saw his face as if for the first time. A stranger? It was as if he was looking over the shoulder of a stranger and seeing their face not his. He shook his head to try and clear it, but it didn't work. The voice in his head, the one he talked to himself with, was oddly distorted. Weird! It sounded different. Distant, as if in slow motion.

The boy had paid. As he saw Michael come from the men's room, he gave him a little smile and started down the stairs. Michael followed. The boy waited at the bottom of the stairs.

Michael stood next to him. He didn't look at him. He daren't. He just looked forward.

"Come on." The boy took Michael's hand and led him round the garden. They didn't speak. Michael saw nothing. He felt totally numb.

"Shouldn't you be back at work. If you're getting a taxi, can I get a lift? I've got to get back to Tech. The Coke people are coming in. It's going to be a little awards ceremony. Cash prizes!"

🦋

Michael somehow managed to get through the rest of the day. Luckily, all he had to do that afternoon was organise the volunteer rotas. Mundane work, but complex enough to occupy his mind. And yet it didn't feel like his mind. He felt totally separated from his mind, and his body. It was the person in the mirror at the tea room who was sitting at the computer. The stranger. He watched from above.

"Are you alright Michael?" Mark put a mug of tea on the desk. "You seem a bit strange! Distant?" He put his hand on the stranger's shoulder.

"Of course he's strange. He's a stranger. How can you not notice, Mark? I'm up here. If you only looked up you'd see me."

🦋

He walked all the way home, from Paddington to Mossman.

A long time since I've walked over the bridge! Michael, or was it the stranger, thought. He stopped half way to stare at the city. Over an hour passed. It grew dark.

"You alright mate?" The joggers voice jolted him back.

"Yes, er, yes. Just enjoying the view."

"You sure?"

"Yes. Really." He carried on walking, staring fixedly at the joggers back as it grew smaller and smaller.

The lights glaring from the opened windows and doors of The Oaks caught his attention. His feet took him in, and the man from the mirror, ordered him a beer. "A schooner of New, with a dash of lime." Michael was surprised that he knew what to order. He bought him another. He drank it slowly then left the pub. When he reached Spit Junction he realised his feet had taken him too far. He made them turn round and take him back along Military Road and home.

The man from the mirror seemed to have keys to Michael's apartment. Michael watched from above as he unlocked the door, let himself in, went for a pee, undressed, and sat on the bed. Michael looked down at his feet. He still had his socks on. They were white cotton but the dye from the insoles of his new shoes had stained them quite a bright yellow on the toes and heels. He stared at them for quite some time, but then he noticed his back was beginning to ache, so he sat upright and swung his legs onto the bed and lay down.

He was suddenly desperate to pee, and to go for a dump, yet he couldn't move at all. He was getting an intense pain at the base of his stomach. His body was altogether too uncomfortable, heavy, like lead.

"Get out," someone said. He floated up and looked down.

The stranger was lying on the bed where Michael had been. The man from the mirror! He got up and walked from the room, but ever so slowly, like a very old man!

Michael sat on the lavatory seat, staring at the stained socks. The colour of pilau rice in an Indian restaurant, he noted. An hour passed, maybe more. The telephone was ringing. He pulled off a strip of lavatory paper and listened to the recorded voice.

"Michael is unable to take your call at the moment, please leave your name and number after the tone and he will get back to you as soon as possible. Bleeeeeeeep."

"Michael wherever are you? Everyone at work is so worried. It's nearly twelve o'clock. Is something wrong? You seemed so odd yesterday. Has something happened?"

🦋

Mark had a key to Michael's flat. At twenty-two minutes past one, he let himself in and was surprised to find a stranger lying in Michael's bed, seemingly unable to move. Michael watched from above.

Mark is so kind, fussing over a stranger as if it was me, he thought.

Mark managed to get the stranger to the bathroom. He even made him sit down while he removed the stained socks.

Showered and dressed somehow, the stranger sat on the settee, expressionless, while Mark phoned for a cab.

Michael watched them go into the medical centre. He sat

The Butterfly Boy

with them as they waited. The stranger still, stiff, silent, staring ahead, hands still, on his knees. Mark flicked through the pages of a magazine, but kept turning to look, concernedly at the stranger sitting staring into space, dressed in clean pressed jeans and a blue checked shirt.

The doctor was young, no more than twenty-seven. He prescribed Prozac.

Michael suddenly noticed the television. He knew that it was meant to be a children's programme, but why was that silly young woman talking to the person dressed as a bear as if it was a half wit. Perhaps she had good reason? The bear, apparently called Humphrey, certainly didn't seem very bright.

Michael felt odd, displaced, somehow very clean and new, but curiously weak. He spun round a little on the settee to investigate his surroundings. Mark was sitting at a small round glass topped table, not his table, engrossed in a newspaper.

"Mark, why am I at your place? What day is it? I don't understand! Why do I feel so incredibly hungry?"

"Oh, thank god. You're back. My dear, dear friend."

Mark jumped up, throwing himself at the settee and flung his arms around Michael, sobbing.

"Rhyme, come here. Michael's... Oh god!" his sobbing increased.

Rhyme appeared in the doorway to the kitchen, wiping her hands on a tea towel. She too burst into floods of tears and rushed over to the settee and flung her arms round him from the other side.

"Oh Michael, I can't believe it. We thought you'd never come back. You frightened us so much. You old bugger!"

She gave him a little punch, then clung on to him incredibly hard, burying her head into his neck. More floods of tears.

"Hey, you're both choking me." Michael actually laughed. "So where have I been? Have I been ill? Why are you staring at me like that? I feel so weedy! What day is it?"

They both just sat back looking at him.

"Is either of you ever going to speak, tell me what's going on? Could I have a drink? I'm really thirsty."

Mark jumped up. "Oh god, yes. What do you want, Michael? Mineral water, herbal tea?"

"Any chance of a beer?"

Mark turned in the kitchen doorway, eyes still streaming with tears.

"Shit mate, you've no idea how glad I am to hear those words. You can have fifty beers if you want."

Rhyme gathered up both Michael's hands in hers, and gazed deep into his tired, black rimmed eyes. "Michael my lovely new friend. Don't you know? You've been really sick. We've been so worried. Mark and I, well, everyone."

"What kind of sick?" Michael faltered, his eyes darkening.

"A breakdown. Doctor Clark, he's been looking after you, said your mind was just overloaded. It just couldn't cope, so it switched off. He put you on Prozac. Said you'd be fine after a while. We believed him at first, but it's been so long." Her eyes welled up with tears again.

Mark returned to sit on the other side of Michael on the settee. He handed him an opened bottle of beer. Michael took a long drink and turned to Mark.

"What do you mean so long? Mark? Have I been unconscious?"

"Not exactly. More like the living dead, like a zombie."

"What d'you mean?"

"Well it's very hard to explain, if you really aren't aware at all of what's been happening. Doctor Clark said you might not remember. For almost two weeks, no *exactly* two weeks, you have been in this zombie-like state. You've slept most of the time. Well, not quite so much for the last couple of days. When you've been awake, though, you've been like a robot, just staring ahead, or at the television. You've done everything we have told you, like a child, cleaned your teeth, eaten, well a little bit, but no reaction."

"Who's we? Who's been telling me to clean my teeth, feeding me, looking after me? Where have I been? In hospital?"

"No Michael. Here, my place, where you are now. We've taken it in turns, a roster." Mark managed a little laugh.

"Who?"

"Me and Rhyme most of the time. Dreadful Damian's done quite a few shifts. I've never seen Damian so serious before. He's been worried sick, too. We all have. Kevin's helped. And the girls. Getting food down you has been the worst. You've got very thin I'm afraid."

"I feel so terrible. How can I have done this to you all? O god, oh why? I can't remember anything!"

"Do you remember me taking you to the doctors?"

"No."

"What's the last thing you remember?"

"I vaguely remember someone talking to me. On the harbour bridge I think? Then a pub? No it's all blurry."

"Michael, try hard. Please. What's the last thing you remember, properly remember?"

They watched him closely. His eyes flashing this way and that, as if watching some scene at high speed. Then he closed his eyes tightly, dropped his head slightly. Tears once more running down his too thin face.

"I remember." He spoke almost inaudibly. "We met in the Chinese gardens." He kept his eyes tightly closed.

"The boy?"

"I think we should leave it at that, Mark," Rhyme gently interrupted. "Michael's remembered. He's back with us. He'll get better now. Darling, you said you were really hungry. Shall we take you out for something to eat. Somewhere quiet. It would do you good if you can face it. To get out, out of here. Do try. Come on. You don't need to talk at all if you don't want to?"

"Yes... Oh, thank you both... Oh, what would I...?"

They all stood up slowly. Michael stared at Mark, then at Rhyme, then flung his arms around them both. They stood holding each other, gently, for several minutes, then Michael pulled away from the group, straightened himself and announced slowly and quietly.

"Thank you both so much. It's all over now. I feel it. I'm going to get well, be strong, start again, properly, sensibly. No more silly emotions. No more tears. I've cried enough for a life time. And now I'm making my friends cry too. It's just too stupid."

By the time they got to the vegetarian Chinese restaurant, which was mercifully quiet, it being still early for dinner, Michael was obviously already exhausted, his face drained of colour.

In the taxi, he had talked non-stop. Talked of going back to work, taking up painting again, getting back to the gym.... Mark and Rhyme humoured him and let him ramble on, but in the restaurant he became silent again and seemed to be withdrawing slightly. He merely picked at his food.

"Michael, you're doing brilliantly, do try and eat, drink some more wine... Michael, Rhyme and I have done a lot of talking while you were, well, off with the pixies."

Michael actually smiled, and visibly softened, relaxed, a little colour returning to his face.

"We think you should get away, from here, from, well, everything, the past, what's been happening recently. We think you should take a trip overseas. You've got plenty of money and Rhyme's aunt...?"

"But I've got to get back to work!" Michael interrupted, suddenly agitated.

"Look, Michael. You've been really sick. The doctor said it could take quite a while for you to get really strong. To properly recover. If you like we'll take you to see him, Doctor Clark, to talk. He's really nice, you'll like him, he'll explain. And Mark's checked up at work, you're well overdue for long service leave. In fact, they are going to give you a year's sabbatical. So now you really can take up painting again. You keep saying you never have the time."

"But where? How?"

"It's all sorted, we're packing you off to the South of France, as soon as you're strong enough to travel."

"Yes, you remember I told you about my mad Aunt Atlanta, well I've spoken to her and she's more than happy for someone to go and live in her little house in Provence. She hates it being empty. There's an English woman, Carole I think she's called, who lives in the same village, apparently. She has the keys and goes in from time to time to air it, but otherwise it's just sitting there empty."

"But I couldn't."

"Yes you could, we haven't gone to all this trouble for nothing. It'll be heaven. The European spring has almost started, and when you're settled in, we'll come over and visit you, in their summer, July or August."

"And then it'll be your turn to look after us and spoil us with lots of gorgeous Mediterranean food and cold rose wine."

"Do you really think I could?

"Yes!" Mark and Rhyme replied in unison. They all laughed and spontaneously held hands around the table.

Part II
Bellejac, South of France

Less than three weeks later, at the end of March, Michael, Mark and Rhyme were at the airport. They had reached the front of the check-in queue.

"How many pieces of luggage are you checking in sir?" asked a grinning Qantas attendant.

"Two."

"No, three. Here, it's a little present from Mark and me. So we can keep in touch. It's a fax and answer machine. I checked and there's phone line at the house. All you have to do is plug it in. It's even got paper in it."

"Oh, thank you both, but will it work overseas?"

"Yes. We've checked that too."

When they had finished checking in Mark said, "There's ages before you need to go through, lets go and get a beer in the bar."

Although Michael had resolved to shed no more tears, his eyes welled up once more when he saw the surprise. All his friends were there waiting in the bar to say good-bye. Damian came up first and gave him a big hug. "Shit, mate, we'll miss you." Then he pulled away and continued, "Can't imagine why, you boring old fart."

Everyone laughed. Kevin came forward holding out a parcel, wrapped in rainbow striped paper and tied with an enormous pink bow. "A little something from all of us, to make sure you keep in touch, you should just about have time to understand the instruction book during a twenty three hour flight."

Michael tore the paper off. "Oh thank you, just what I've never wanted."

"You'd better use the fuckin' thing," Damian laughed, "you've no idea how difficult it is to buy someone else a mobile phone. Thank god for the gay Mafia, and me being so young and gorgeous and persuasive. It's all charged up and ready to go, so no excuses!"

🦋

By the time Michael got out at Bangkok he was actually beginning to feel really excited. The flight had been great so far, particularly as he had treated himself to a business class seat. The food was better than he had anticipated and the copious amounts of champagne had induced a blissfully long sleep. He walked quickly down the seemingly endless halls full of duty free and souvenir shops to stretch his legs.

His cabin crew from Sydney walked past, dragging their little suitcases on wheels and joking with each other. One of the stewards, who had been particularly attentive during the flight, turned and gave Michael a huge wink and a grin. On the strength of this mild flirtation, in a moment of sheer madness, Michael bought a huge chunky G Force watch for himself. "Completely not me! But maybe the new me, the South of France me, wears things like this?" he joked with himself.

Michael arrived at Heathrow very early, took a taxi straight into London and checked in at the Basil Street Hotel in

Knightsbridge, which had been recommended by Rhyme. He spent the morning wandering around the shops. Everyone seemed very friendly. It was bright and sunny but very cold. Harvey Nichols was nice and warm. Cosy almost, after the crowds of noisy tourists in Harrods.

The lift to the fifth floor smelt of rather too much expensive perfume. It was still only eleven thirty. "What time is that in Australia, who cares, that's the past!" he thought, then sat on a bar stool and ordered a glass of champagne.

Three glasses of champagne and two plates of Japanese rice crackers later Michael could hardly keep his eyes open. He dragged himself back to the hotel, which was mercifully just around the corner, and fell into bed. His phone went at three o'clock. His alarm call. He felt like hell. As if he could sleep for ever. But this was his only day in London, and he had only ever been once before, with David. He made himself get up, and after a shower and a cup of Earl Grey tea he felt ready for anything and took a black cab straight to the British Museum.

David had loved the British Museum, they had been back two days running, and poured over the drawings on the ancient Greek vases. The taxi came to a halt outside the metal railings.

"Anything wrong guv? This is it, yer actual British Museum. We're 'ere."

"Umm... look, I'm really sorry. I've changed my mind. Could you take me to Soho instead." He quickly flicked through his notebook. "Old Compton Street, please."

Michael spent a very happy afternoon drifting from café to shop to bar. Everyone was so friendly. In a shop called Prowler he bought a copy of *Gay Times* magazine and asked the boy who served him where he could get something to eat.

Balham's was lovely, bright jolly and friendly, like a big party. The waiters were all gorgeous, and knew it, continually flirting outrageously with all the customers, almost all of whom were male. The restaurant was packed and Michael squeezed onto a tiny table by the wall.

"Hi, where are you from?"

Michael immediately liked the two boys at the next table.

"I'm from Sydney."

They were from somewhere called Leeds, just down for a couple of days. One was a hairdresser, and his boyfriend it turned out had been the winner of Mr Gay UK a couple of years before.

Michael decided he loved England, well London. He wished he wasn't just staying one night. Still he could come back whenever he wanted. He had all the time in the world. He could afford it. In fact if he was reasonably careful he needn't ever work again, if he didn't want to.

His new friends took him everywhere or so it seemed, never staying in one place for more than one drink. They ended up in a crowded pub called Compton's, where just before eleven o'clock, the barman called 'last orders'. Michael resisted the temptation to be taken on to a club, even though he wasn't as tired as he felt he should be, but his flight to Marseilles next day was very early.

Addresses and phone numbers were exchanged, and Michael sensibly took a taxi back to Knightsbridge.

The Butterfly Boy

Michael was surprised that Marseilles airport was so chic and modern. He had expected something much more old fashioned. On top of which it was called Marseilles-Provence, which made it seem even more glamorous.

Even though he had plenty of French cash on him, he tried his card in the cash point machine, just to see if it really would work. Out spat one thousand five hundred French francs. It seemed unbelievable, that here on the other side of the world all he had to do was poke a bit of plastic into a hole in the wall, punch in four numbers and money came straight out of his bank account in Sydney!

He ordered a beer, in French. He was pleased. His accent didn't sound too bad, he thought. He sat at a shiny silver table with his trolley of luggage next to him. He checked all his papers, found the voucher for the Budget hire care, the map and instructions on how to drive to the village.

He looked around, drinking it all in. Life was at last beginning to look very rosy. He felt his whole body relax, as if knots were being loosened. At the table to his right a blonde woman of indeterminate age, dressed in white jeans, gold cowboy boots and a tight low cut tee-shirt embroidered with sequins and bits of fake fur was brushing the small dog on her knee with one hand and smoking with the other. Her long fingernails were the brightest red Michael had ever seen, as was the lipstick border on her coffee cup.

Michael turned his head. By total contrast, the young woman at the table to his left wore no apparent make up. She leant with one elbow on the table, head resting on her hand and holding her long brown hair back from her face. She was totally engrossed in what appeared to be some kind of text book, occasionally writing in a note book. Stopping for a second, she sat up, staring into space, deep in thought. Then she seemed to become aware that Michael was studying her, and turned towards him. They exchanged smiles. Michael felt a warm little glow. The friendly gesture, made him feel at home, relaxed, wanted. He decided he was going to like France.

As he wheeled his trolley full of baggage out of the airport the warm air hit him like a friendly slap on the back. He hadn't expected it to be quite so hot. He pulled off his sweat shirt and headed, smiling for the Budget office. "Time to test out my French properly!" he thought.

🦋

After driving north for about an hour and a half, he turned off the motorway. Rhyme's instructions were perfect. Should he ring her? On his new phone, try it out. No, it's the middle of the night in Sydney isn't it? Anyway, new life, new me, keep looking forward, he speculated.

The road was narrow and winding, climbing upwards through stunning rugged scenery. The low hills were covered in short scrubby undergrowth. Leaving the motorway Michael had opened the windows. The cooling breeze was laden with heady unfamiliar smells. Intoxicating. Not a soul in sight. For twenty minutes or so no sign of human habitation. He pulled off the road for a minute, to inhale the green herby perfume and watch an eagle circling overhead.

The road wound down to run along the side of a shining river, then through a couple of small villages, the houses built from stone. He could hardly believe how picturesque it all was, so French! Then as the landscape became flatter the road passed through small fields of vines. The neat perfectly pruned rows dark against the dry looking earth, splattered with brilliant green from the first leaves.

The road sign read Bellejac 5 K. His new home, only five kilometres away! He stopped by the road again. He took out his new mobile phone, looked at it nervously, then dialled the ten digit number which Rhyme had neatly written down on his instruction sheet. It was ringing, but it sounded odd. Was that the engaged tone or did they have a different tone in France?

"Bonjour, Carole ici."

"Bonjour, er, Carole, this is Michael. Are you expecting me?"

"Hello, Michael. Yes of course I'm expecting you. Rhyme phoned last night to confirm that you were on the flight. Where are you now, Marseilles?"

"No, I'm five kilometres from Bellejac. I've just driven through a tiny village called St Roch. And a big camp site along the side of the road."

"God, you're only a few minutes away. That was quick. Look, drive into town. Well, it's a village but officially it's a *ville* not a *village*. You'll see the church. You can't miss it. There's a square with a fountain. Park the car anywhere. I'll meet you there with the key in fifteen minutes."

Michael was spellbound by the tiny town, it surpassed his wildest hopes. How could anywhere be so incredibly picturesque. It looked like a film set. The square was not even slightly square, but a long rectangle, surrounded on three sides by stone buildings, At one end a large imposing church was topped with an oversized statue of the Madonna silhouetted against a piercingly blue sky. Facing it at the other end of the Place de l'Esplanade was a massive square, severe-looking building which must surely be the chateau. Along one long side of the Place was a higgledy-piggledy row of buildings, which included a small restaurant. The outdoor tables covered in Provencal printed cloths and the glaring white umbrellas made Michael smile with anticipation of the meals he knew he was going to enjoy there. All the buildings had window boxes filled with red and pink trailing geraniums. They were not the same as the ones in Australia, these seemed more open, almost lacy looking, he noticed.

A low stone wall ran along the fourth side of the Place where the land fell away steeply. Beyond the wall was a breathtaking view across a wide fertile plain to a distant row of low mountains, which seemed to change colour even as Michael looked.

In the very centre of this fourth side of the Place a large house divided the panorama in two. It had no front garden of any kind, the front door, like those of all the all the other buildings opened straight onto the pavement. The house was three stories high with five windows across the top two floors and two tall windows either side of the double front door on the ground floor. The windows were all tightly covered with wooden shutters, painted a pale mat lavender colour, which, Michael thought, looked so perfect against the honey-coloured

The Butterfly Boy

stone. Apart from the exceptional beauty of the architecture, this grand residence stood out from the more modest houses in that its window boxes were empty. No geraniums!

Michael leaned back, resting his bottom on the circular stone wall of the fountain basin. The stone felt smooth and deliciously warm against his hands. Had it once been used by the village women for washing clothes? he wondered. He dipped his hand in the water and splashed his face.

The square was totally empty. Not a soul in sight. Where is Carole? he thought, suddenly a little nervous. Michael stared fascinated at the house. Then either side of it at the view. How far away is *my* house? he wondered. He was itching to come back and sit on the low wall and paint the view, the ever-changing mountains.

The sun was making him sleepy. His eyes began to close. But suddenly he was aroused by the sound of hard heels clicking on stone. A figure emerged from the dark open doorway of the church. A woman of sixty or so, Michael guessed Maybe more? She was dressed in a long droopy black dress, with a black scarf tied around her head and lots of silver jewellery. Her slightly eccentric outfit was made even odder by the fact she wore shabby, tall black leather boots with very high scuffed narrow heels.

"Hello, you must be Michael. Have you been waiting long? I didn't hear your car. I was miles away. It's so peaceful in our lovely church. Do you want to look inside? No, I suppose you want to just get settled in. You'll have loads of time for exploring. Atlanta wrote to say you were staying indefinitely?"

"No. I mean, yes," Michael laughed. "I mean, no, I don't

know how long I'm staying, but certainly for the summer, and yes I would love to see inside the church. I'm in no hurry. A gentleman of leisure." He laughed again, and followed the clicking scuffed stiletto boots into the dark cavernous interior.

"Isn't it lovely? I come in here a lot. It's seventeenth century. Rather grand don't you think for such a small town? The windows are later, but very lovely. Look there's Saint Francis. You don't see him often in windows. You don't see him very much at all in Catholic churches in fact! I've always had this theory that he was secretly never very popular with the church hierarchy. All that giving away your belongings to the poor and living with the lepers. A bit of a hippie? A bit too much of a socialist? I love him, being poor, you see!" She laughed. "He's my friend. I come in here to talk to him. Look, you must light a candle. You know you get a wish? That's if it's the first time you visit a church. Some say three, but I think that's being greedy. Our candles are particularly efficient, so be careful what you wish for! Have you got any small change. Five francs?"

"Yes, no, a ten franc piece, enough for two. Here have one on me."

The coin made a hollow metallic clank. He thought of the screen door, the shack. He shivered.

He took a tall tapered candle from the tray beneath the tiered candle holder, lit it from one of the already burning ones and forced it onto one of the spikes on the top row.

He knew he shouldn't! He tried not to, but he made the wish anyway. He shuddered again.

"Come on it's cold in here, let's get you into the house."

Back in the sun, standing by the fountain Michael regained his equilibrium. "I'll be fine. It'll take some time. Doctor Clark said I'd be fine," he tried to comfort himself.

"Well, what do you think of your new home?"

"Where? Oh, no. It can't, it couldn't!"

Michael followed the limp dress and clicking heels across the square. Carole took a huge bunch of keys out of a large bag made from some kind of faded ethnic embroidery. She put the largest one into the key hole of the lavender front door. The black metal knocker Michael noticed was in the shape of a woman's hand, bordered with a lace cuff and holding an apple."

"But Rhyme said it was a little house!"

"Wait till you see the gardens on the other side, they go on for ever. Unfortunately, Pierre, the old fellow who's done the garden and the odd jobs for years, has just done something awful to his back. I'll have to find a replacement. It shouldn't be too difficult. There's massive unemployment round here. I'll just put an add in the window of the tabac."

The door swung open into a large square entrance hall with a sweeping stone staircase pale wooden grandfather clock and enormous crystal chandelier.

"Oh, god, it's like a dream!"

"We need to get all these shutters open, get some air through. Yes it's divine isn't it. Seventeenth century, like the church, I think... And Atlanta's got such perfect taste, and money. Just one of those paintings would set me up for life,"

Carole sighed.

The house was exquisite. Each of the countless rooms was decorated with French antiques, mostly eighteenth century. The walls in many of the rooms were covered in elaborate hand printed wallpapers. Everywhere, the thick curtains were draped and swagged, with elaborate borders of fringe and *passementerie*. The dining room was particularly grand with pale wooden panelled walls and a long polished table surrounded by twelve high backed chairs. There was a strong smell of furniture polish.

"Raphaella comes in once a week to do the housework. She's Spanish. Her husband's the local carpenter. They've lived here over twenty years, but the locals still all them 'the foreigners'. Atlanta pays for all that, and for the gardener, but if you want to pay Raphaella extra she'll come in as often as you want. She'll do all your washing and ironing, and even cook if you like?"

The salon was Michael's favourite room. All yellow, its walls were papered in a large antique Chinese design and the curtains were of heavy dull yellow silk. In one corner stood a grand piano and next to it an elaborately gilded harp. Above the grey marble fireplace a dark ancient-looking mirror, speckled with black, reached almost to the stone vaulted ceiling. Above it a rectangular painting of ladies in eighteenth century costume walking in Chinese garden. On either side of the deep mantelpiece, stood two oriental figures in brilliantly painted porcelain. Opposite the fireplace, two sets of French windows opened onto the terrace and sprawling gardens. Michael opened one and gazed down in disbelief.

The Butterfly Boy

An odd clicking noise behind him made him turn. The room was empty. Carole, it seemed, was busying herself in the hall beyond. He could hear her shoes. The clicking noise again? In the breeze from the open windows, the heads of the porcelain figures swayed and rocked swayed on hidden hinges. They seemed to be laughing! With Michael or at him? He peered into the dark mirror at the design on the papered wall opposite. A tiny distant figure appeared to be running, chasing something, with what looked like a tennis racket in his outstretched arm? He turned and walked across the room to take a closer look. The little figure wore Chinese mandarin's robes. The tennis racket was a net. Above it, just out of reach, a butterfly. Michael shuddered. A sudden gust made the yellow curtains rustle. The figures on the mantelpiece rattled. He didn't turn but walked straight out into the hall.

"There, it's going now. Isn't it a lovely comforting sound, like the heartbeat of the house. A resuscitated heart!" Carole explained how and when to wind the clock. "Now down here is the kitchen. It's lovely. Atlanta always used to eat breakfast in here. It gets the morning sun. There's a new gas cylinder in the cooker, it was the last thing Pierre managed to do. In fact I shouldn't wonder if it wasn't how he injured his back.

"That's the thermostat. The water's on constant and the heating will come on for a couple of hours twice a day. It's hot now but it gets surprisingly cold at night. The instruction books for that and the washing machine etc. are in this drawer. Now, I've put some milk and butter in the fridge. There's tea and sugar and some honey in the cupboard, and a baguette in this." She lifted the lid of a long lidded wicker basket, attached to the back of the door. "The bread lives in here. Not very hygienic, but very traditional! I've put the receipts under the kettle. It's electric. Kettles of any kind are quite a rarity in France, believe it or not. So you're lucky!"

The receipts were all carefully pinned to a piece of ruled note paper where Carole had scrawled a column of figures and added up the total. Michael quickly settled his bill. Carole seemed overly-grateful, he noted with interest.

Half an hour later, the rest of the house explored and explained, Carole stood in the open front doorway. "Well, I'll leave you to unpack and settle in. What time is it? Oh just four, the clock's chiming. How funny. Look, if you want I'll meet you at about six thirty, walk you round the town and then perhaps we could share a pizza. I'm sure you won't feel like cooking tonight. I'd offer to make dinner for you, but frankly I'm a lousy cook. I basically live on scraps. Eat like a bird really."

Michael observed the well rounded hips filling out the shapeless dress.

"That would be great if you can spare the time. You can fill me in on all the local gossip. But couldn't we eat at that pretty restaurant over there, rather than go for a pizza?" Michael was secretly disappointed to discover that this dream village actually had a pizza restaurant. It certainly wasn't part of his fantasy.

"Well... actually, you see it's rather expensive, and I...!"
"Look, it's my first night. Let's have a treat. It's my shout."
"What?"
"Sorry it's an Australian expression. It means I'll treat you."
"Well, if you're sure you..."

"Of course I've...,Of course, please let me."

"I'll book for seven thirty then, as I walk past. I'm pretty sure Yvette's in. The door's open. Oh, if you need me, I've written my phone number on the back of that bit of paper I gave you. Or just knock on my door. It's just round the corner. I've got a tiny flat, a cupboard really, above the Assurance in the Grand Rue."

Michael was quite pleased to see Carole go. He was sure she was nice enough, but suspected she could be quite clinging. He immediately decided on a strategy. He would explain that he was here on doctor's orders. To find total peace and quiet. His painting would be a good excuse too. His lips formed an involuntary mischievous smile.

He walked around the house again exploring every room. He noticed many more details now that he was on his own. He adored it, his new home, his new life. His suitcases seemed extraordinarily heavy as he dragged them up the curving stone staircase. He was conscious that the wheels could chip the worn stone treads.

He had had no difficulty in choosing which of the seven bedrooms he would sleep in. It was at the back of the house, on the first floor, overlooking the gardens, with the view of the mountains. More importantly, however, it was different from all the other rooms, being totally white and quite plainly decorated. The floor was dark polished wood, but every thing else was white. A huge wooden four poster bed was hung with the same coarse white linen, as the simple floor length curtains. A hand stitched white quilt was neatly turned back to reveal white embroidered linen sheets, and huge square fat pillows over a long round bolster. A small chandelier hung from the white plastered vaulted ceiling. The only other furniture in the room were two white painted round tables on either side of the bed. On one, stood a curly black metal candlestick with five cream candles, on the other a very ancient looking leather-bound bible. On either side of the bed, beyond the tables were two panelled doors. One led into a tiny modern bathroom, and the other into a dressing room with capacious built-in cupboards and drawers.

The only other simply decorated room in the house was large attic on the top floor with very little in it except for a large wooden table and some empty suitcases. Old Louis Vuiton ones. Michael couldn't quite believe that they had just been left there. He could just imagine how Damian would shriek if he saw them. He would write tomorrow, well, fax tomorrow, and tell everyone his adventures so far, he decided. The room was very bright. Perfect for painting, he thought. It would be his studio and study, he decided with childish delight. Unaccountably, there was a phone socket in this seemingly unused room, as there was in every room, including his bathroom. He set up his new fax on the wooden table, and next to it in a neat row, his lap-top computer and printer. My own new little office, he smiled to himself.

The Butterfly Boy

Michael was slightly disappointed that they had to sit inside the restaurant that evening, but it had turned surprisingly cold. as soon as the sun went down. Colder than he had imagined it would be in the South of France. Carole wore an almost floor-length, hand-knitted, woollen patchwork coat over the same black dress. The green squares stood out, as they alone were covered in rough bobbles. She chose the most expensive menu, the one with foie gras. "Could I really? You're sure it's not too expensive?" Much to Michael's amusement she ate like a horse, even finishing off Michael's rich chocolate and chestnut desert.

They finished off the evening with coffee and brandies in a café looking out onto the square on the other side of the village.

Carole let Michael pay for the drinks without any protestations this time.

"That's where they play *boules*, the men. Under the plane trees. You'll see. Stupid game. But then, so are French men. Well, most of them. Yes, I know it sounds racist, but you'll see! Oh, is that the time. I've got to get up early. A house in another village. Swiss people. I look after it when they're not there. I look after quite a few houses you know. The pool people are coming in to install a new filter. Got to keep an eye on them or they'll probably chip all the tiles.

"Oh, Michael, it's our market day here tomorrow, Friday. You'll love it. It starts at nine. Don't get up too late, they pack up at twelve."

Richard Cawley

Michael woke just before seven. It was still dark. He snuggled down, luxuriating in the slightly rough linen sheets, which still smelt of being recently ironed. The clock in the hall chimed seven times, and then a few seconds later chimed another seven times. Michael smiled to himself. By the time he had shaved and showered, it was morning. The mountains looked like glass in the early grey light. The sky seemed vast, very high. Pale blue, with a few wispy clouds over the hills.

He made some tea. While the kettle boiled, he unlocked and opened the kitchen door. It immediately made the room quite cold, but he wanted to feel, to smell the air. The bread, he was surprised to discover, was already quite stale. He toasted some under the grill and spread with it with hard butter from the fridge and honey. It tasted wonderful. Mug in one hand and toast in the other he walked out of the door onto the gravel terrace. His feet crunched. He lifted a white painted metal chair from a stack and sat down at a round metal table. The top was perforated all over with small holes. A larger one in the centre was obviously intended to accommodate a sunshade. He wondered if there was one. And if so where it might be.

He hesitated, thought, for a moment then brushed the dust from a patch of the table, then put is toast down on the clean patch. He took another sip of tea then warmed both hands on the mug. The metal chair seat was surprisingly cold on his bottom. He stood up again. The garden beckoned. "An enchanted garden?" he pondered. It seemed to lure him. Entice him to discover it's secrets. He put down the mug on the table. Stone steps led down onto a broad perfectly manicured lawn. As he looked behind him to see the back of the house for the first time he noticed how distinct his footsteps were in the dew on the grass. He was pleased. He was beginning to make the house, the garden, his own. Like a cat peeing on new territory. Beyond the lawn a gravel path wound through a tall shrubbery, almost maze-like. And beyond, to Michael's delight and astonishment, a formal Chinese garden, just like the ones on the wallpaper in the yellow salon. There was lots of bamboo and rocks with a small lake shaped like a figure of eight. Michael stood on the wooden bridge, painted in black and dark red, which spanned the narrow part of the water. Between the water lilies, enormous orange fish swam slowly backwards and forwards. On the other side of the bridge, set to one side was a small open-sided octagonal pavilion, with a curving pointed roof. Michael walked up the three wooden steps and looked through the open circular entrance. A bench ran all round the inside. Leaning against the wall, was a large dusty white umbrella, covered in spiders' webs. Michael smiled.

Behind the Chinese garden a dense thicket of white pampas grass hid a large vegetable garden, and beyond that another empty plot of bare earth. Finally the grounds were enclosed by a tall stone wall, almost covered with fruit trees, which were perfectly trained so that their branches stretched out horizontally and parallel, flat against the wall. Two thirds of the way along to the right was a wooden door and beyond that the rest of the wall was covered by a lean-to green house filled with garden tools and neat stacks of pots.

Michael walked back towards the house. A shaft of sunlight

made a bright patch on the wooden bench in the Chinese pavilion. Michael sat in the warm pool of light and sighed peacefully. He straightened his back, closed his eyes and placed a hand, palm upwards on each knee.

※

He picked up the toast. The tea was stone cold. He went inside and made a fresh pot. The clock chimed once. What did that mean? he wondered. He walked into the hall. Nine thirty! he noted. The market would have started! he realised.

He pulled on his denim jacket, removed the big black front door key from the bunch hanging on a hook just inside the kitchen door and walked into the hall. Then he remembered, and dashed upstairs for his mobile. Then up another flight to make sure the phone was on 'out', and the fax switched on. Oh shit, there's no message on the answer machine! he agonised, I'll do it later, no one's going to phone me this morning. I mustn't miss any of the market.

Michael had always thought of himself as having a good sense of direction, but he couldn't even begin to remember the route which Carole had taken to the square on the other side of the village. He got lost twice in the maze of tiny stone-paved alleyways. Twice he came back to the same little square with a tree in the middle. On one side was a pizza restaurant, but it looked very firmly shut up, as if it had been shut for months.

Then, following a tiny lane which ran through an arched tunnel, under a very ancient looking house with a round turret, he came out onto a much wider street. Lots of people were bustling in and out of the various shops. The Grande Rue? he guessed. Most people seemed to be walking in the same direction so he followed them. Oh, there's the bread shop! he noted. There was a queue. It smelt so good. I'll get some the way back, he decided. I wonder what time they close?

Michael suddenly found himself back at the café where Carole had taken him the night before. Several people were sitting outside in coats and thick jumpers, drinking coffee. Much to his surprise a few of the older men were already drinking glasses of red wine. The sun still didn't have much warmth in it although the sky was piercingly blue and cloudless.

The market was a dream. Just as Michael had hoped. Twice he took heavy plastic carrier bags of food back to the house. He knew he was buying far too much, but he simply couldn't resist. Everything looked so wonderful. He had never seen vegetables like it. There were huge piles of asparagus everywhere. Green, like Australian asparagus, and a different sort, fatter and almost white. He bought half a kilo of each. And cheese! He hardly ever ate cheese at home, yet he bought three different sorts from one irresistible stall. Further along, a tiny stall was decorated with photos pinned to the front of the brightly coloured printed fabric which covered the table and which showed a picturesque farm and lots of white goats. He bought a day old goat's cheese. Chalky white and soft, still oozing liquid from its perforated plastic container. The stall holder, a big smiling man with long hair, a beard and earrings explained that these really fresh cheeses were delicious eaten sprinkled with sugar or even honey.

Michael immediately bought two different kinds of honey,

lavender and chestnut from the next stall. The honey that Carole had bought for him, he realised, was obviously from a supermarket, and off no specific variety. The stall was manned by a young hippie-looking couple. He talked to them for quite a long time. They were so friendly and interesting. He learnt that they lived almost an hour away in a hilly region called the Cevennes. Their house was high on the side of a mountain, with lots of land where they grew most of their own food. They were vegetarians, although not vegan as they ate some dairy produce and kept bees for honey.

As well as keeping bees they made tie-dye tee shirts and tops from natural dyes, which they sold to tourists in the summer when the markets were apparently much, much bigger. They wrote down their address and phone number and invited Michael to come and see the bees. They seemed so genuine friendly and it all sounded so idyllic, particularly the remote mountain pools which they promised to show him.

As they were talking, Michael noticed a blaze of colour out of the corner of his eye. Brilliant scarlet. He turned and smiled. Geraniums, a few stalls further along. There seemed to be no one manning the stall however. Should I come back later? he wondered. Then, just as he was about to cross the road to the café opposite, a different café this time, the Bar du Midi, a young man in denim dungarees over a thick dark red shirt appeared out of a dilapidated white van behind the stall.

"Can I help you?" he asked in French, but with a strange almost Italian sounding accent.

"Yes, please," Michael replied. "Some of these, well, lots actually. I don't know the name for them in French?"

"Are you English?"

"No. Australian."

"Oh, I've never met an Australian before! That's why you're so tanned. The sun is always shining in Australia isn't it? How many? Which colour?"

Michael laughed. "Well, not always. It even rains sometimes. Just the red please. No pink ones. How many? Oh, I don't know." He thought quickly. "At least thirty pots, no forty!"

"My god, so many! Are you going to take them back to Australia?"

"No," Michael laughed again. "I'm living here for a while. Well, several months at least, and my house, well, it has so many windows!"

"Here in Bellejac? I'll give you discount, of course. Well, it is such a big sale."

"Yes. It's a large house over near the church. Place de l'Esplanade."

"Would you like me to deliver them, in the van when the market closes?"

"That would be very kind."

"Not, it is you who are so kind Monsieur. I never expected to sell so many plants in the whole morning, well all week at this time of year!"

Michael paid and walked over to the café, sat down and ordered a Café au lait. When the waiter brought it back, he noted that he referred to it as a Grand Creme. Michael's first lesson in modern colloquial French!

As he sat drinking his coffee, he studied the young man as

he stooped, sorting out the plants. He wasn't very tall but was stocky, with very broad shoulders. His shiny black hair was quite long and fell in a thick fringe over his eyes as he bent forward. Occasionally he would brush it back from his face with his hand. Beautiful hands, Michael noted. But rough and stained looking on the insides. He stood up, and caught Michael's eye, giving him a wide grin. His incredibly dark eyes flashed. He was certainly very handsome, in an unconventional kind of way. Wide high cheekbones. Russian looking almost? Quite wild looking! Gypsy? About twenty-eight, twenty-nine? Michael speculated.

Several times he looked over at Michael and grinned. No? He couldn't be interested in me. He's just pleased to have sold so many plants. Anyway he's obviously straight. Although he did comment on my being tanned? Straight blokes don't usually comment on each other's appearance! Still this is France. Maybe it's different? Michael smiled inwardly.

As he left the café, the plant man grinned again.

"See you later. By the time I've packed up it'll be about twelve-thirty or so. I'll drive straight round. OK ?"

Michael bought marinated olives, a litre of olive oil, some wine from a local producer and a neat bunch of new season's garlic, before he arrived back at the first café, where he ordered a beer.

He was pleased to find the bread shop still open as he walked back along the Grand Rue. He bought a long loaf with unusual very pointed ends. The day was quite hot now. He planned a feast of asparagus for lunch. It was quite warm enough to eat on the terrace. Michael felt a huge rush of plea-

The Butterfly Boy

sure, contentment, lighten his whole body. He quickened his pace.

✤

"Do you have a shop?" Michael asked the plant man as he lined up the pots to one side of the front door.

"No, I just do the markets. Every morning except Sunday."

"What about the afternoons?"

"Oh, not a lot. I do a bit of gardening for people. When I can get the work that is, but there's not much around at the moment."

Michael's heart jumped.

"Otherwise I just pick my little boy up from school if I'm not working."

Michael's heart sank.

"You're married?"

"Yes, Claudine. We were very young. She's got a good job. In the post office in St Stephan."

"St Stephan?"

"Yes, it's the next town. Twelve Kilometres. You've never been?"

"I only arrived in France yesterday!"

The plant man laughed. "I see. Of course. Well, it's where you go to shop. There are two big supermarkets. You can get anything in St Stephan. It's nice. It's not a village like Bellejac. It's a proper town. I live there. The only drawback is we have no garden. I would love a proper garden to look after."

"Look, this is totally crazy! It's such an unbelievable coincidence, but I'm looking for someone to do the garden here. I would have to check with someone else, to make sure she hasn't already found someone. I can't imagine she would have though. Give me your phone number."

Michael sat at the white metal table on the terrace, he pushed his plate with the debris of his asparagus feast to one side, poured himself another glass of wine and picked up his phone.

Carole seemed pleased with his news at first, but then seemed rather agitated.

"Look, Michael, this is a bit embarrassing, but would you do me the hugest favour? If Atlanta mentions this gardener business, would you mind just inferring, you don't actually have to lie, that I found this new guy? You see, it's kind of what she pays me for, doing all that stuff."

Michael agreed and hurried inside.

He pulled the grubby bit of paper out of his back pocket with the telephone number scribbled on in thick pencil.

"Hello. Excuse me but are you the man I bought the geraniums off this morning? I'm the Australian. I forgot to ask your name."

"Yes. It's me. I'm called Bruno. Bruno Picot. You are Monsieur...?"

"Michael, just Michael, please. Look, Bruno. I really do need someone to look after my garden, if you're still interested?"

Bruno was obviously very interested indeed and drove straight back to Bellejac to inspect the garden and agree on details and terms.

It was agreed that he would work Monday Wednesday and Friday afternoons starting the following week. Michael thought the hourly rate Bruno asked for was ridiculously low. Much less than Carole had said. He was going to insist on paying for the gardener himself while he was in residence. Atlanta was being more than generous anyway letting him have the house rent free. After all she had never even met him.

Bruno insisted that it was enough and also suggested a month's trial period. He seemed incredibly grateful for the work.

The days drifted by and the weeks rolled into one. Michael was happier than he could remember. Once a week he took Carole out to dinner. She wasn't too bad. Occasionally he drove her into St Stephan to do a supermarket shop.

Several times he drove up to the mountains and stayed the night with Phillipe and Marie Ange, his new hippie friends, invariably going to bed very late, very drunk and stoned. They seemed to be genuinely fond of him, treating him almost like a pet. In return, on Fridays, after the market, he would cook lunch for them. His French and his cooking improved rapidly.

He discovered and fell in love with nearby Nimes, Arles, Orange and, in particular, Avignon, where he discovered a bar with a rainbow flag outside. The gay couple who ran it soon became friends and invited him occasionally for Monday lunch. In low season they closed the bar one day a week. He also discovered an excellent art-supply store in one of the winding back streets not far from the bar.

Most days when he wasn't exploring, he would drive into the countryside with his sketch books and water-colours. As the days grew longer and hotter, he would often drive down a dusty track to the river to paint. After a picnic lunch he would take off all his clothes and sleep in the sun, to recover from the effects of the wine.

There was never anyone to disturb him, except, as spring began to turn into summer, canoeists would occasionally glide past him on the shining river. No one seemed even slightly bothered by his nudity, but as their were several naturist campsites in the vicinity, he supposed the locals were quite used to it.

He took up riding lessons at an equestrian centre he discovered in the nearby countryside, where immaculate stables surrounding an enormous house which had once been a Cistercian monastery.

Matthieu, the riding instructor, was a dish. Michael advanced from one to two lessons a week. Matthieu told Michael he was an excellent student. He seemed to give Michael more attention than the others, constantly checking his posture. On one occasion he told Michael that he should sit on the horse like a prince. Michael was enchanted.

He also planned to take up the piano. The one in the yellow salon was in perfect tune. Carole said she thought she could find someone to give him lessons. Charlotte, the young music teacher from the local school. There simply weren't enough hours in the day, or enough days in the week.

The Butterfly Boy

His phone never stopped ringing, and the faxes would arrive almost daily, or nightly, until his friends got used to the time difference! Everyone phoned and faxed, but mostly Mark and Rhyme. Often they would write joint faxes. Michael was so pleased that they obviously got on so well together.

Past troubles were never mentioned. Only bright optimistic local news and gossip. Damian, it transpired, had fallen in love, and had been seeing the same boy for over three weeks!

Michael sat at his computer at least twice a week and wrote back. He related every detail of his new French life. It was going to make an excellent diary, a book perhaps?

As planned, Bruno came three times a week, working much longer hours than he was paid for, and as the evenings grew longer, he would still be working away until seven o'clock in the evening.

Each afternoon, around five, Michael would take two small bottles of cold beer into the garden. They would walk around, bottles in hand and Bruno would show Michael his progress. They would have a short chat, on pre-ordained subjects, the weather, the increasing number of tourists, the state of business on the market. He never once mentioned his wife or child. Michael in turn never enquired, but he found this odd and was also surprised that Bruno never ever asked anything about his own life, or why he was there? Perhaps he considers it improper to pry into an employers personal affairs? Michael supposed.

Sometimes they would sit in the little Chinese pavilion, out of the sun to finish their beers. Often they sat in complete silence. it wasn't an uncomfortable silence. On the contrary it was very comfortable, peaceful, intimate almost.

One Friday, after the had been sitting in silence for several minutes, Bruno gave a little nervous cough, then spoke.

"Well?"

"Well, what?"

"It's finished. The month. My trial period. How have I done? Have I passed the test?"

"Oh, Bruno. Don't be silly. Of course you have. Anyway we're friends now, aren't we?" He smiled at the gardener with affection.

"You're so kind." The gardener looked deeply into Michael's eyes. Then very slowly and gingerly, he stretched out his hand, brushing Michael briefly and softly on the side of his face. Michael quickly caught hold of the hand, pressing the palm to his cheek, then kissing it. His skin was very rough.

"Bruno, I never thought... not for a minute... I mean... do you...?

Bruno nodded slightly, never shifting his obviously adoring gaze from Michael's face.

"Bruno are you sure? I mean, you might?"

Bruno nodded harder. "Please!"

Michael walked back up through the gardens, turning occasionally to look back with concern at the gardener who followed several paces behind. He was wearing the same dungarees he always wore, but with no shirt. His serious face and muscular arms were wet with sweat and smeared with dirt. his heavy boots, caked with earth. Looking like that, Michael mused, he could be a porno star.

By now Michael was feeling unbelievably excited, but was worried nevertheless. Oh god, should I be doing this? He's just too nice. And he's married for god's sake, with a kid. It's probably the first time? He's going to hate himself afterwards, he agonised.

The gardener followed Michael into the house, stopping purposefully to leave his muddy boots by the kitchen door, then followed him up the stairs. Michael had hardly closed the bedroom door when Bruno grabbed him by the shoulders, span him round, and began to kiss his mouth so hard and passionately that Michael thought he was going to faint. They fell onto the bed, onto the white quilt, tearing at each other's clothes.

Afterwards, they lay back panting for a while, then to Michael's surprise, Bruno pulled back the quilt and the top sheet.

"Get in, please."

They lay in each others arms for almost an hour. Bruno constantly stroking and patting Michael and covering his face with the gentlest of kisses.

Suddenly he sat bolt upright, and looked at his cheap watch.

"Oh shit, it's twenty past seven!"

He jumped out of bed dragging on his clothes.

"Do you want a shower?"

"No time... Michael?"

"Yes. Are you alright?"

"Did you mean what you said?"

"What?"

"About us being friends?"

"Yes, of course I meant it. But... we're more than friends now!"

"Michael?"

"Yes?"

"Please... No one must know."

"Of course... I promise, Bruno."

"Michael?"

"Yes my friend?"

"Can we... I mean... again?"

"If you're sure you want to. Yes, whenever you want."

"Michael?"

Michael laughed.

"Yes Bruno?"

"Do you... do you have... a special friend, in Australia?"

"No I don't Bruno. I did once. But I don't now."

Bruno grinned.

"Until Wednesday."

And he was gone.

Michael suddenly noticed the state of the white bedding. Oh god, how am I going to explain this to Raphaella? I'd better get a badly behaved dog quickly, he thought, laughing out loud, then walked over to the window, gazing out smiling. "So it was an enchanted garden!" he said aloud.

☙

The days grew very long and the early mornings and evenings

The Butterfly Boy

much warmer. Michael could not have been happier. He bought several large canvasses from the art shop in Avignon. Raphaella's husband, made him a beautiful wooden easel, and he began work on a series of large oil paintings, working in his attic studio, from his water-colour sketchbooks.

One Sunday afternoon, while he was sketching by the river, the town's young mayor walked past and stopped to chat, admiring his work. The next day he called round to the house to see the large canvasses, and asked Michael if he would like to have an exhibition in the chateau. The town always held an art exhibition of some kind, every year in mid-July to coincide with the local fête, but the artist who had been going to exhibit that year, had recently decided to go and live in Morocco and cancelled at the last minute.

Michael loved the idea. He suspected he might not sell much work, but he wasn't bothered. He didn't really need the money, after all. But it was a goal, something to work for. And then he could ship the paintings back home later, and maybe have an exhibition in Sydney.

Michael's' circle of friends increased, his French continued to improve and three times a week he made love with Bruno, usually in the white bedroom, but occasionally if they simply couldn't wait, in the Chinese pavilion. Once they tried the greenhouse, but it was unbearably hot. Life was perfect.

🦋

Then one Sunday the phone rang just before four in the morning. Odd. They all know the time difference between here and

Australia, Michael thought with irritation. The phone stopped ringing and Michael could hear the noise of a fax coming through. God, I hope no one's ill! He rushed upstairs and read the fax as it came through. His blood ran cold.

Michael
I have been trying non-stop to get this number out of your friends. I heard you had been ill. They are all so protective of you. I think they blame me. Anyway my persistence finally paid off.
Your friend Kevin eventually gave in.

I'm so sorry you've been ill. I was devastated when I heard you'd gone away. I've been a stupid self-centred boy. I wanted to have my cake and eat it. I got it all wrong. I think about you all the time. I know it's probably too late. You probably hate me. Or more likely you've forgotten me, but I think I'm in love with you

Please, please, please write back. Even if it's just to tell me to fuck off!

No signature, just a little drawing of a butterfly.

Michael picked up the phone straight away. He knew the number by heart. It was imprinted on his heart. His pounding heart. He must be there. He had just sent the fax. If he didn't do it immediately he would chicken out, he decided.

The Butterfly Boy

Eleven days later Michael drove to Avignon. His mind was once more in a complete turmoil. Why was he doing this? It had all been going so well. He had been so happy. So contented. He had almost got him out of his hair. Well almost? Was he mad? he wondered.

Mark and Rhyme certainly thought he was. They had heard the news immediately! Sydney is very small when it comes to gossip. Particularly on the gay scene. Oddly the fax was just from Rhyme, not Mark. He must be totally pissed off with me. I bet they won't come to visit now. Not if the boy's here, Michael worried.

The train was due at two fifty-five. Just before one o'clock, Michael parked his car in the open air car park just outside the city walls, a little way down the road from the station. The Arab boy gave him a ticket. Michael stroked the Alsatian dog which lay outside the door of the little wooden office. The dog didn't get up. It was used to Michael by now.

The flight was direct from Sydney to Paris. Then the fast train straight to Avignon. He'll be tired! Michael fretted.

He had given the boy his credit card details over the phone. He could just imagine how disapproving Mark would be if he heard! Fortunately the boy had a month's break from college, starting the next week. He had taken a few extra days off so he could fly immediately.

Michael walked through the stone walls into the beautiful little city. He had come to love it so much. It will all be different now though! Oh god, is this all going to be a mistake? No the boy had said the words. Put them in writing. 'I think I'm in love with you!' He agonised again.

His friends in the bar were supportive, but seemed concerned. They knew the whole story. They didn't lecture him though. The day was incredibly hot and leaning on the bar, talking worriedly, Michael downed four beers in a short space of time. He wasn't thinking. And he was sure to have another one when the boy arrived. Oh shit! The French police were so strict. There was no way he could manage without a car! His mind rattled on.

He walked back to the station along a back road, where he remembered seeing a small hotel. He booked a double room and paid in advance.

At first he thought the boy wasn't on the train. He began to panic. Then he caught his first sight of him coming up the stairs behind a group of scruffy looking young kids with back packs. Michael's heart leapt. Although the boy also was carrying a large back pack, he didn't look even slightly scruffy! He looked totally divine, wearing his habitual, neat minimal clothes. This time in a white tee shirt and dark brown knee-length shorts.

The boy saw Michael and grinned, holding out his arms. Michael tried to hug him, but it was almost impossible with the back pack. They both laughed. They didn't kiss, but it all felt so natural, so right, so comfortable, so much easier than he had imagined.

"Drink?"

"God, I'd kill for a cold beer!"

"Let me take your bag?"

The Butterfly Boy

"No. It's fine, I'm used to it. Anyway it's not that heavy."

They walked across the busy road and through the city walls.

"Oh god I can't believe it. It's so amazing, is this where your house is?"

"No, it's in a village. Well, a little town really. An hour away. Look, the police here are even stricter than in Australia and I've already had quite a few beers, so I've..." Michael gulped, "I've booked us into an hotel. We don't have to stay the night. Just..."

The boy stopped and laughing, turned to Michael. He grinned.

"Michael, you are so funny. It's totally cool. Anyway you don't think I could possibly wait as long as an hour to shag my boyfriend!"

Boyfriend! He had said boyfriend! Michael thought his head was going to explode from sheer pleasure.

"We can have a drink here."

They sat opposite each other at a small table on the pavement, sipping their beers and smiling into each others eyes. The boy talked non-stop. Firstly about the journey, then asking endless questions about Michael's life in France. Suddenly he stopped talking, gave Michael a particularly affectionate little smile and took hold of both his hands across the table. An elderly woman at the next table, with tightly permed hair and a pale blue patterned sleeveless dress, tutted loudly. The boy flashed her a look, then took Michael's head in both hands and kissed him long an hard on the mouth. He gave the woman another defiant look. She tutted loudly again and looked the other way.

"Another drink?" Michael giggled.

"I'd rather have a shag." The boy laughed. "Anyway let's leave the stupid bitch to enjoy her drink in peace."

"Au revoir," the boy said pointedly to the woman as they edged past her table. She tutted again.

"You speak French?"

"Yes, quite well in fact, or so my teachers told me. I've always been a natural mimic. I've never been to France though. This is my first time. To Europe."

The spiral staircase was very narrow. The boy had difficulty getting up with the back pack. The room was small, with a lavatory and shower screened off by a flimsy partition in one corner. While the boy was showering, Michael undressed and sat on the bed. It was an ugly room. Michael wished he had booked in somewhere nicer. But the Hotel du Commerce was out of the way and seemed discreet. The walls were covered in a striped flocked paper. Mustard. Why do the French have such terrible taste? Michael wondered. It was a constant source of amazement. The partitioned cubicle was covered in the same ugly mustard paper. Michael opened the window. The windows of the house opposite had all shutters closed, he noted with pleasure.

He removed the brown quilted nylon coverlet, folded it neatly and put it on a shelf in the wardrobe. The sheets were plain white. Michael bent down, they smelt freshly ironed.

"I've tried my best, but I can't stop the shower dripping!"

"We won't notice," Michael smiled.

The Butterfly Boy

It was just past ten-thirty when the boy woke up again. Michael hadn't slept at all. He just lay there smiling to himself, cradling the sleeping boy in is arms. Watching the pulse in the smooth slender neck make the silver chain tremble slightly with every heart beat.

The shower dripped constantly. Michael didn't care. He had thought himself happy for the last couple of months. It had been nothing. Life had just begun!

There was no one at the reception desk. He was thankful. He just left the key on the desk.

They stopped in the same café on the main street, and ordered two *croques monsieurs*, toasted ham and cheese sandwiches. Michael ordered a glass of champagne for the boy, and an alcohol-free beer for himself. They remembered the tutting woman from earlier and got a fit of giggles. Michael ordered another glass of champagne for the boy. I will buy enough champagne for him to take a bath in if it will please him! he decided.

At the car park the Alsatian got up and walked over to Michael wagging its tail. The boy held out his hand. The dog immediately licked it enthusiastically as if he already knew the boy well.

"Wait here for the change. I'll go and get the car."

The boy dumped his ruck sack in the boot and climbed into the passenger seat. As he was fiddling with the unfamiliar seat belt Michael studied him adoringly. Suddenly he noticed something which made him take a sudden involuntary intake of breath.

"Your earring? The butterfly?"

"It's gone. I lost it. Woke up one morning and it just wasn't there!"

"Can't you get another?"

"No, it was a present. From a jewellery student. He left last year. I have no idea where he is now."

The boy was as enchanted with the house, the village, France, Michael's new lifestyle, as Michael had hoped. He fitted in instantly. It was all too easy. Michael's new friends all fell instantly in love with the boy. Carole alone seemed a little wary at first, prickly almost. Jealous perhaps? Michael wondered, but he knew the boy would quickly win her over.

The boy talked to Raphaella, as he did to everyone. After just one meeting, Michael saw that she would have rolled over and died for the boy.

There was only one problem with the butterfly boy's integration into Michael's new life. Bruno!

Michael had decided to be honest with him. The Wednesday before the boy arrived he had told him, the truth, everything, as they drank their beers in the Chinese pavilion.

Bruno had seemed to take the news quite well. He had finished his beer in silence, given Michael an odd, sad little smile and said. "I had better finish my work then..." and disappeared behind the tall hedge of pampas grass. That Friday he didn't turn up.

The Butterfly Boy

The following Tuesday, Raphaella arrived for work out of breath and obviously very agitated.

"Oh, Monsieur Michael. It's terrible. That poor young woman. And the child. It's awful. They seemed so happy. No real money problems now. No one can understand why?"

Michael blanched.

"What Raphaella? Who? What are you talking about?"

"It's Bruno, Monsieur."

"Oh god! What has he done?"

"Nothing. Well I don't think so. No one knows. He's just gone. Left. No note. Nothing! It must have been another woman! Oh, his poor wife. He seemed so nice, so docile... so happy?"

Raphaella burst into tears. Michael put his arms around her. He was relieved at the distraction. He could think of nothing to say. He couldn't let himself think about it. He had suffered enough. It was his turn now to be happy. He tried to put it out of his mind. He went to look for the boy.

🦋

Life went on as before. It was all too easy, too perfect. Everyone as usual was instantly charmed by the boy, who seemed somewhat calmer than before, Michael thought. He fitted in so easily, and although he still seemed able to cast a spell within seconds over everyone he met, he now hardly left Michael's side. Whenever they were alone, he would hold Michael's hand, kiss him. In public he would throw him secret affectionate glances.

Richard Cawley

The joint faxes resumed from Mark and Rhyme, once more, filled with all the light hearted news and gossip from Sydney. They never however mentioned the boy. In return Michael didn't elaborate on his new love affair, saying no more than "we" did this or that. Mark and Rhyme planned a visit in September. Presumably they imagined the boy would have long returned to college in Sydney by then?

Carole found a new gardener, Monsieur Thassy, a retired gendarme. His relationship with Michael was polite but formal. The boy would often wander in the now lush gardens. He adored them. Michael however, now seldom ventured further than the terrace. The boy couldn't understand it or why he always refused to visit the Chinese pavilion with him. He seemed to sense a certain unease and soon stopped mentioning it.

The exhibition was looming closer. Raphaella's husband made wonderful frames from old oak beams. Totally simple, very rough and primitive looking. The boy helped Michael frame the pictures and hang them. He also arranged huge vases of flowers which Monsieur Thassy reluctantly allowed him to pick from the gardens. By this time the boy had worked his charms on the elderly black clad Monsieur le curé, who allowed him to borrow several large vases from the church. Monsieur Thassy didn't mind the boy cutting the pampas grass so much, but was deeply shocked that the boy insisted on hacking long branches from the ancient headily scented wisteria, which was blooming for the second time across the whole back of the house. The boy also made Michael drive him along a small road which led out of the back of town, to cut enormously long stalks of wild fennel, which grew along the side of the road. The lime green of the lacy tops contrasted brilliantly with the pale purple hanging wisteria flowers.

The room in the chateau was vast. The ringing mobile echoed loudly. They both jumped, then laughed.

"Yes, this is Michael."

"Michael daarling, its Atlanta. How are you daarling? How's my little house?" She had already phoned several times before. She seemed incredibly friendly, if a little eccentric.

"It's time we met. Enrico's having a party next week. You'll love him. It'll be divine. He adores Australia. Bring your little friend. I'll get Franco to fax you a map and details. Come the day before. The party's next Thursday. Bring something nice to wear. There'll be lots of interesting people."

Before Michael could speak, she had hung up. How extraordinary! he thought, how did she know about the boy? Rhyme? Were they checking up on him? Getting Atlanta to spy? Still it might be fun. The boy would love it, a trip to Italy. They could leave really early, in the morning, stop off for an hour or two in Nice, Monte Carlo?

The following day was Sunday, and the opening of the exhibition. The reception was at six p.m. Michael had paid Carole to organise the invitation list, and was then to employ her to man the reception desk for the month of the exhibition. She was thrilled to have the extra income. Particularly as she was also to receive five percent of the price of any painting she sold.

Another five per cent was to the mayor's restoration fund for the chateau's much needed new roof.

The party was great fun and very noisy. At first the guests made a little pretence at examining the paintings, but seemed to be more interested in the social aspect of the occasion, and the free aperitifs. Nevertheless, much to Michael's surprise and delight, four of the large works had red spots on them by the time everyone left the party around eight. Three had gone to the Swiss couple, whose swimming pool repairs Carole had supervised. She introduced them to Michael. They were pleasant and complimentary, but very formal and proper. The husband was a eminent psychiatrist and his wife, a Freudian analyst. As Michael was chatting to them, he became aware of a strong smell of marijuana drifting over the polite little group. He turned to see the boy, dressed in thin white embroidered Indian top over loose white linen trousers drinking Pastis and sharing an obviously hand rolled cigarette with his hippie friends. Michael tried not to smile.

The fourth large painting was bought by a retired Dutch couple who had a *maison secondaire* just outside the village. Michael had never spoken to them before, but they always gave him a nod of recognition whenever he saw them in either of the two cafés he frequented. They, like Carole, were somewhat prone to droopy, arty looking black clothes and silver jewellery. Their clothes however, unlike Carole's, always looked brand new, and expensive. Oddly Carole, who seemed to know most people's business, had little to relate on the Dutch couple other than the rumour that he was an unsuccessful poet, and that the locals were convinced that they both practised black magic!

There was also a red spot on one of the small water-colour sketches that Michael had decided, at the boys insistence, to exhibit at the last minute. It was a tiny study of the river, very early in the morning. It had been intended merely as a colour note for a larger oil, but the boy thought it was wonderful. Michael was flattered to discover it was the mayor who had chosen it. He decided to give it to him as a thank you present.

Raphaella was one of the last to leave, splendid in a lurid blue artificial silk suit with a floral blouse and matching hat, obviously bought for some wedding in the past. Her face almost as red as the Martinis she had been drinking so enthusiastically.

"I'm so proud Monsieur Michael. Oh, Monsieur Michael!" She burst into tears and flung her arms around his neck. "If only Bruno was here. He would also have been so proud. I think he was very fond of you. He admired you so much, I know. He always said you were so kind to him."

Michael was greatly relieved when her husband, also red-faced and shuffling, put a strong affectionate arm around her and said. "Come on, ma chere we have stayed too long. Stop being so emotional. Thank you so much Monsieur Michael. It was good. I am proud to have made the frames for your beautiful pictures. I must admit I thought it was a strange idea at first, to use the old wood, but now I think I understand? Yes I think they really work. Come on old girl, I think we need to take you home and get some food down you if you plan on going to the fête later. Au revoir."

When the crowds eventually dissipated, the noise of the

fete, gathering momentum on the other side of the village, gradually began makes itself obvious. The throbbing beat of the loud techno music, forcing its way through the narrow winding streets of the village to the chateau seemed strangely incongruous.

"Oh, Michael, come on. Do let's go. We don't want to miss the band. Apparently they're awesome. We can eat later, and I can't wait to punish you in those dodgem cars."

The hippies seemed just as enthusiastic about enjoying the pleasures of the fête, but Carole was less so. She became quite frosty in fact.

"No, thank you, Michael, really not quite my scene, all that loud music and all those common people. I'll stay here and clear up." As she spoke she was making a terrible mess, attempting to transfer the contents of one half-empty bottle of wine into another. "Well, it's a shame to waste it! I'm going to put my ear plugs in and have an early night. I think I can feel another of my migraines coming on!" Michael had noticed that Carole's 'migraines' usually coincided with occasions when she was able to avail herself of free alcohol! He smiled inwardly.

The whole of the big Place, down the steps from the strip of ground opposite the cafés and shops, where the men played *boules* was throbbing. It seemed everyone from the town and surrounding villages, except Carole, was out to enjoy themselves. An open air *buvette* provided beers and soft drinks and hot chips. There were fairground stalls and rides of every description, each competing with each other to play the loudest pop music. The dodgem cars won hands down. Michael's

The Butterfly Boy

little group stood around the barrier for a while, drinking cans of beer, smoking joints and watched the local youth attempting to give each other spine damage as they crashed their little cars into each other.

"Come on, Michael, lets show them how Aussies drive!"

Michael gave the boy some money and he dashed to buy tokens from a young woman in a gaudy blazing kiosk. Close to she wasn't so young, but wore her blonde hair pulled tightly back in a long pony tail. She wore a tight leopard skin corselett and extraordinary elaborate eye makeup.

They stayed on the dodgem cars for several rides, and as usual the boy acted as an instant magnet, so that within seconds all the young kids were laughing and joking with him and vying with each other to bump his car.

At ten exactly, the band started. Michael had seen nothing like it. There were about twelve performers who seemed capable of singing dancing and paying every kind of musical instrument. They changed costumes with every number, which ranged from Abba to opera to the latest heavy rock numbers. There were twelve enormous video screens, laser light shows and clouds of dry ice.

The show was so spectacular, it was the kind of thing Michael would have expected to see in a large Paris theatre. The crowd went wild and the party atmosphere grew noisier and happier.

Michael couldn't remember when he had so much fun. The boy persuaded him to go on every ride, even the most gruesome. They gorged themselves on trashy food and beers, and smoked endless joints. By the time they finally exchanged affectionate farewells with the hippies it was almost two in the morning.

Michael walked back through the village with his arm around 'his boy'. He didn't care who saw them. He assumed that everyone, except perhaps dear Raphaella, had put two and two together by now. They sat in the yellow drawing room with one last beer, then tottered drunkenly up the grand stone staircase to the white bedroom and made slow sleepy love. The perfect end to a perfect day, Michael thought as he fell asleep with a smile on his face.

"Menton sounds lovely." The boy was reading a guide book. "This says it is more old-fashioned and less spoilt than resorts like Nice and Cannes and St Tropez. Have we time for a look?"

They had set off just after six in the morning.

"Yes, but that will mean we'll probably only have time for a quick stop of in either Nice *or* Monte Carlo, not both."

"I've just got this feeling about Menton. I've never heard of it before. Everyone back home has heard of the big places, but Menton..."

"OK, if we just keep going without stopping off for coffee, we should get to Monte Carlo by eleven. We can only have a short stop though, or we won't get to Menton in time for lunch. I really doubt we'll have time to see Nice though?"

"That's cool with me."

The view of Monte Carlo, glittering in the morning sun, way below the service station, where Michael stopped to refuel, was breathtaking.

"Wow. Amazing. I never imagined it would be that small. So that's where Grace Kelly lived!"

They stopped in the middle of town and drank very expensive coffees in a glitzy café. The boy stared at a group of four mature women gossiping at the next table. They were dressed to kill, looked as if they had just stepped out of the hairdressers and all wore lots of obviously real jewellery.

"Not like Bellejac this, is it? More like Double Bay back home in Sydney. Do you have to be old to live in Monte Carlo?" The boy giggled.

"No, I don't think so, but you definitely have to be very rich. We might as well look have a quick look at the shops while were here. Not too long though if you want to spend some time in Menton."

Michael stopped to look in the windows of Cartier. His heart skipped a beat. "Oh god!" he muttered. The boy didn't hear, he was engrossed in trying to discreetly photograph a tottering, ancient looking woman, whose miniature poodle was dyed the same bright lilac as the pompadour hairstyle.

He walked over to Michael.

"Did you see that? The dog actually had a Gucci collar on. It said 'Gucci dog,' unreal! Michael we can't go in there. Not in Cartier dressed like this!"

The doorman had already opened the door. The boy followed Michael warily inside the shop. Michael didn't know where he was getting the courage from. Perhaps it was because this was the first time he had ever seen the boy not quite his totally confident self. In fact he was obviously quite nervous.

"Bonjour messieurs." The severe looking woman behind the counter gave them an all-too-obvious up and down look, paused briefly and continued in English. "Is there anything I can help you with?" She gave her immaculately tailored navy pin-striped jacket a little tug at the hem and let out a faint nervous cough.

"Yes." Michael was surprised at his own voice. It sounded surprisingly confident and assertive. He was pleased he was wearing his TAG watch, not his new G Force! "The earrings in the window." He turned and pointed. "I would like to see them."

"Oui, Monsieur. Of course."

The boy threw Michael a quizzical look. The woman returned with the earrings. Michael noticed that for all her immaculate grooming she had unfortunately thick ankles.

"Oh, god, Michael, you can't. You couldn't!"

"How much are they?"

"Eighty thousand francs Monsieur. Diamonds of course, in white gold. In American dollars that's let me see..." She took a calculator from under the counter.

"Actually we're Australian."

"Oh, excuse me, Monsieur. I thought... Let me see..." Her demeanour had softened noticeably. Michael's assertive attitude seemed to have convinced her that he was serious. "That's in the region of, well it's about twenty thousand Australian dollars."

The boy, frozen until then, let out an audible gasp.

"Could you split them? I only want to buy one." He looked sideways at the boy. The woman softened even further. Her whole body seemed to relax slightly. She gave Michael a barely perceptible smile.

"Well, it's not usual Monsieur. I don't know. I must speak to the manager. But I'm sure we could get one made for you?"

"No, that's no good. I want to buy it now. To take it away."

She seemed to be gone for ever. Michael's heart was pounding. He pretended to look at watches. The boy sat frozen in a chair by the counter, staring at the glittering little objects.

"You're lucky, Monsieur. He's in a good mood. He was successful at the casino last night. We can get another one made to replace yours. To make a pair again. And meanwhile we have one more pair for the vitrine, sorry, window." She actually grinned as she took Michael's gold card. She disappeared to the back of the shop.

"Michael, no! You can't. I won't let you!" The boy actually had tears in his eyes. Michael resisted the temptation to grab hold of him.

"Shut up!"

The woman came back with the small strip of paper. Michael signed.

"Shall I wrap it, Monsieur?" she unclipped one earring and held it, tiny but blazing with light in her hand. "Or would?" she glanced quickly at the obviously dazed boy and then at Michael with a knowing little grin.

"Well?" Michael looked at the boy.

"I don't know. I mean should I? I mean, is it alright? Oh, Michael!"

"Of course, Monsieur. This is Monte Carlo. There's no point in owning diamonds if you don't wear them." She walked towards the boy unclipping the back of the earring. "There Monsieur, look in the mirror. It looks wonderful I think. Quite splendid... But at the same time discrete. Not too ostentatious. Monsieur looks very well... But then Monsieur would look good in anything!" She flashed Michael a knowing look. Michael watched the boy's expression in the mirror, as he turned his head backwards and forwards slightly, making the tiny butterfly blaze and flash.

"Oh, Michael!" He jumped up and flung his arms around Michael's neck. Michael could feel the warm tears through his thin shirt. "Oh Michael, thank you."

The woman was positively glowing as they left the shop. "Au revoir, Monsieur. You have excellent taste." Another knowing little look, almost saucy this time. Michael forgave her her thick ankles. "Au revoir, Monsieur. It looks well, in the daylight. You are very fortunate to have such a generous friend young man! Au revoir, Messieurs. Bon chance. Bon apetit."

The boy was totally silent in the car as they drove along the coast in the direction of the Italian border. Michael smiled to himself, as, out of the corner of his eye, he watched the boy's hand constantly moving to his ear, fingering the butterfly. He knew he was resisting the temptation to pull down the mirror and admire himself. By the time they got to Menton, he seemed to have got over the shock and was back to his old chattering butterfly self.

Even though it was still not quite high season, it took ages to

The Butterfly Boy

find a parking space. It didn't matter, the boy seemed terribly excited, child-like almost, by his first view of the Mediterranean. The day was a scorcher, the sea shimmered and dazzled, as if to compete with the diamond butterfly. They eventually found a perfect shady spot under a tree right by the sea at one end of the promenade, above what seemed to be the most popular part of the beach for swimming. Behind, picturesque houses, with different coloured bright shutters, clustered together up the hillside.

"Shall we bring our swimmers?" the boy was delving in the old Vuiton suitcase he had persuaded Michael to let him borrow. He had insisted that if Atlanta was lending the house she wouldn't mind him borrowing the case.

"I don't know if we'll have time, not if we have lunch?"

"Well we needn't have a full menu. We could just quickly eat one gorgeous little plate of something? Please, Michael? I've never swum in the Mediterranean?"

Michael laughed, giving the boy a playful squeeze on the scruff of the neck.

"You know I won't say no to anything you ask, you little tart. Let's have a quick look round the old town then find somewhere to eat. Sandwich do?"

The boy flashed Michael a mock disgusted look. Michael laughed again.

"Come on then, tart."

The boy was almost skipping he was so obviously happy, flitting from shop to shop, peering into courtyards and photographing details of antique door knockers, peeling paint on old shutters, quaint lace curtains and window boxes.

"Oh, Michael. Look!"

"We really haven't time!"

The crowded little square was lined with small restaurants, the tables and chairs spilling right over the pavements onto the road. The space in the middle was crowded with makeshift stalls, covered in antiques and bric-a-brac.

"Come on, this looks nice, let's eat here. There's an empty table."

A smiling waitress immediately brought menus, adjusted the sunshade.

Michael ordered red mullet with black olive tapenade, and the boy ordered a Salad Niçoise. The waitress came back quickly with bread and a dish of tiny black olives, a bottle of Badoit, sparkling mineral water for Michael and a carafe of rosé for the boy.

Michael sat back in blissful contentment, nibbling on the bread and olives and watching adoringly as the boy, wine glass in hand, wandered around the stalls. His boy, his beautiful beautiful boy! He couldn't believe it. The boy was indeed looking at his best. He had recovered his perfect tan and all eyes were on him. He had taken off his tee shirt and tucked it into the back of his baggy navy blue shorts. His golden torso gleamed with youthful good health. A few people, Michael noticed, looked a little shocked as they noticed the boy's bare feet. He had kicked off his sandals and left them under the table. But as usual, faces lit up as he stopped at each stall.

Just as the waitress brought the food, the boy came rushing up to the table.

"Michael, please could I have some money, only one thousand francs, I want to buy *you* a present. I've seen something..."

Michael laughed and opened his money folder.

"Look, here's more, then you don't have to keep asking. Don't want you going short. I mean, I don't want you having to pawn your jewellery!"

"Oh, Michael you've already been too...!"

"Shut up, and hurry up. Come and eat your food! I'm going to start, it looks delicious. I'm going to have a glass of your wine. Sod it, it can't be more than an hour or so to Atlanta's, and we don't have to be there till six-ish. A swim will sober me up. I'll order another half. Do you mind red?"

"Do my back for me, please." The boy handed Michael the orange plastic bottle of Lancaster sun lotion which Michael had bought for him in a pharmacy in Monte Carlo. He hadn't quite been able to believe that sun tan lotion could cost that much. The colour of the bottle, Michael noticed was exactly the same orange as the boy's towel and tiny swimming trunks. He had been surprised at the colour of the swimming costume. He had been sure it would have been black, or perhaps white.

"Oh god, I can't swim wearing this!" The boy's hand flew to his ear. "Michael, get me the box, please. It's in your bag."

"We'd better not swim together then." Michael leant close and whispered into the boy's ear.

The beach was incredibly crowded, with people lying almost on top of each other. The two blonde boys lying next to them hadn't stopped staring ever since they arrived. Michael didn't quite like the look of them. They were a bit too good-looking, and their towels and bags and shoes all looked very cheap and worn.

"You go first."

Michael watched the boy wading through the crowds in the shallows, then getting smaller and smaller, as he swam out towards the floating wooden diving platform, moored quite a long way from the shore.

Michael laughed, when the boy, about half way to the platform, stood up, the water not even coming up to his waist. He turned to wave. There must be a sandbank, he decided.

Michael turned to look at the two blonde boys next to him. They were lying on their backs, eyes closed, a Walkman between their blonde heads, one single earphone in each of their ears. He lay back, closed his eyes and drifted off into blissful sleep.

He was woken up by the boy, laughing, and shaking his wet hair, dog-like, over Michael's hot chest. Michael reached out to check that his bag was safe. He looked inside. Everything was OK. The blonde boys had disappeared. The turquoise umbrella and the shabby towels were still there, and their bags, and the Walkman. It was still playing. A faint tinny beat was coming out of the earphones. He turned and saw them heading up the beach towards the cold drinks machine. One, tall and athletic looking, the other, smaller, but almost the same shape, like the same model, in a smaller size.

Michael pulled himself up onto the glaring white painted floating platform by the metal ladder. He felt completely refreshed, exhilarated. Half way across, when he reached the

The Butterfly Boy

shallow bit, he had turned and fixed a spot in his mind. A marker to be able to head back to, when he returned to find his place on the crowded beach. It was easy. The patch of bright orange, just to the right of the turquoise umbrella, directly below the house with the green shutters.

He lay on is back, resting on his elbows, enjoying the sun and watching the antics of the group of young teenagers who were already on the platform. He watched amused as they dived and splashed each other. The boys trying to throw the girls into the water. They can't have been older than fourteen or fifteen. He was charmed by their puppyish rough and tumble way of flirting. He looked at his watch. Almost four thirty! he noted with a start.

He reached the sandbank and stood up. "The green shutters. Yes. The patch of orange. Yes. But no turquoise? They've gone, those boys!"

They hadn't, however. As Michael reached the shore he saw the two blonde boys, bags on their shoulders, crouching on either side of the butterfly boy as he lay stretched out on the orange towel. As soon as they saw Michael walking up the beach towards them, they stood up.

"Ciao then. Maybe some other time?" He heard the taller one say as they turned to head back up the beach. The smaller one who had had the umbrella tucked under one arm, put it up, and laughing loudly, carried it over his head, as they picked their way among the hundreds of brown bodies.

"What did *they* want?" Michael instantly regretted his words. His voice had sounded almost angry.

The boy laughed.

"Michael! Are you jealous? Well, so you should be. Can you believe it? They actually wanted me to go off with them, for a threesome. They were German. But I told them I was quite happy with my rich boyfriend. Oh, Michael, don't look like that. I was joking. About the rich boyfriend, that is. But you have been so generous Michael. I do love you."

"Do you?.. Sorry. Come on."

※

Franco's map and directions were perfect. Not long after they crossed the border into Italy, driving along the narrow Via Aurelia, along the coast, way below the roaring motorway, they saw the sign for the village. A narrow lane filtered off to the right, then under the road and continued to wind it's way up the dusty olive covered hillside until after about half-an-hour they saw the house, set on its own just before the village.

They couldn't miss it! It was as extraordinary as Rhyme had described. Painted a deep dusty pink, with lots of elaborate details picked out in white. It looked enormous, like a Disney vision of an Italian palazzo, with domes and turrets and balconies, surrounded by tall dark pointed cypress trees.

"God, this looks like fun! Better get my earring back in. Shit, I look rough!"

At the boy's request, Michael stopped the car on the drive just inside the elaborate white and gold gates. The boy jumped out, opened the boot, and quickly struggled into a pair of pale grey long cotton trousers and a loose white cotton shirt.

"How do I look? You look great as you are."

Michael already had on long trousers, beige, and a proper shirt.

As the car crunched to a halt on the gravel in front of the extraordinary house, a man in a white livery with gold buttons came out of the front door to greet them.

"Bon giorno, Signore. Signora Atlanta is expecting you. I'm Franco."

The servant wasn't that young, Michael observed. Older than me? Ridiculously handsome! Franco was big, dark, and Mediterranean looking. He's hardly given the boy a second glance. Must be straight! Michael surmised.

"Give me the keys, Signor. I'll park the car in the garage and take your bags to your room. Go into the house. Carla will take you to the library."

Michael and the boy both gasped and looked at each other. The massive octagonal entrance hall was draped in dark tartan. From the centre of the ceiling hung an enormous blazing chandelier made from deer's antlers. Around the walls, between the tall windows, stood a set of huge matching antler armchairs upholstered in tartan. In the centre of the room a massive octagonal table was supported by gilded legs in the shape of griffins.

The table top was an intricate marble mosaic depicting a Scottish highland scene.

In front of the table stood the plainest woman Michael had ever seen. She wore a surprisingly thick pleated grey skirt, reaching below her calves, and a prim white blouse, fastened securely at the neck with a small cameo brooch. Her wiry black hair was parted to one side, tucked behind her ears, and held in place across her low forehead with a plain brown hair grip. Her eyes were oddly large and bulbous. She wore no makeup.

The woman smiled, dropped them a small curtsy and then, without speaking, turned and walked through an arched doorway at the back of the entrance hall. She turned and smiled. Again they followed down a long panelled corridor painted in deep blood red. Between the seemingly endless succession of carved wooden doors on either side of the long gallery, gilded arms with black hands reached out from the walls clasping gilded torches, each topped with a blazing glass 'flame' The woman stopped in front of the last door on the left, opened it, stood to one side and beckoned them with a sideways nod of her head to enter. The door closed behind them.

There she was: Atlanta, an extraordinary sight, reclining on a spectacularly wide brown suede settee in front of a book-lined wall.

Immediately, without any greeting or preamble of any sort, the vision launched into a high speed monologue in a deep gravelly voice with slight American accent.

"Smoke? No, of course not!" She took a Davidof cigarette out of its distinctive silver and wood grain packet and wedged it into a short black holder. "What do you think of Carla? A picture isn't she? No competition there, eh? She's a dream actually. Deaf mute you know. I brought her back from New York. Although she is actually Italian! Used to work for a great friend of mine. Always used to stay with her. Dead now! Poor Charlotte. Stroke. She, Carla not Charlotte, and Franco, are my only living-in staff now, I've got an absolute army of women who come down from Dolcinguetta do all the real work nowadays. In the past I've had an endless succession of gorgeous young boys. Lovely to have around, decorative, but frankly, darlings, they were more trouble than they were worth. Always more interested in servicing each other than being of service to me! Now I just have Franco to look after me!" she chuckled. "Pay him a fortune, just to make sure! Oh, darlings, how rude of me to prattle on. It's just so nice to have company, someone to talk to. You must be exhausted, after the drive. It's so hot. I'm sure you're thirsty. I won't insult you by offering tea. It's too late in the day for anything non-alcoholic, anyway tea's so vulgar, so bourgeois don't you think? A nice cold beer? No, I think we should celebrate." She put the silver whistle which hung round her neck on a black silk cord to her lips. The sound was ear piercing. "She can hear that, oddly. It's about the only thing she can. Oh, sorry I do go on rather. Elizabeth, my daughter, you know, Rhyme's mother, says she doesn't know how I've got to this age without wearing my mouth out. Now, you're Michael. And this... yes, of course, I quite understand. Now come and sit by me, both of you." She swung her long incredibly thin legs down to the floor and patted the suede cushions on either side of her.

The door opened, Carla entered, and dropped a silent curtsy.

"Champagne, Carla, for the boys. I won't. I'll have... no, what time is it? Yes, I'll have my usual g. and t."

Atlanta put the cigarette holder to her lips and looked at Carla with slightly raised eyebrows. Carla picked up an enormous jade table lighter and lit the cigarette, shaking her head in a disapproving way. Atlanta inhaled deeply, then coughed until her frail-looking body shook. The smell of the smoke began to overpower the heavy scent of jasmine perfume, which had pervaded the room until then. Atlanta stooped coughing and patted the settee again.

"Come here boys."

Michael walked across the room slowly, drinking in the extraordinary vision. Atlanta was dressed in a simple beige suit of the thinnest tweed, edged in black braid and heavy with gilt buttons, under it a finely pleated chiffon blouse of the same colour. Around her neck as well as the whistle, she wore a long dull gold chain punctuated along its length with cut crystal beads. The end of the chain was tucked, fob-like, into one of the braided pockets of the jacket. Her immaculately coiffed, chin length bouffant hair, was flicked outward at the bottom and held back from her face and secured behind her ears by a fine black silk scarf. It was impossible to guess her age. She was obviously extraordinarily old, yet still very striking looking, beautiful, even, in a rather scary kind of way. Her smooth skin, stretched tightly over magnificent high cheek bones, was pearly white and without a blemish. Her large eyes framed with an immaculate outline of black kohl, were of a startling pale green. Only her hands gave her away. Long and pale, weighted down at both wrists with several bracelets of heavy pearls. The hands and wrists were spotted with dark freckles, and the heavily ringed fingers, were knotted by obvious arthritis.

"That's it Michael, make your self comfortable. Here boy, oh, I see you've already met Gable. The boy stopped to pick up a small dog with long silky hair, beige, exactly the same colour as Atlanta's. He walked over to Michael smiling, holding the dog out in front of him.

"Look, Michael!"

The dog's collar was decorated with a metal panel engraved with the words 'Gucci Dog.' The dog's breath made Michael almost choke. Atlanta noticed his reaction.

"Sorry, darling, he's terribly old. He's the latest in a long line of Gables. Number one was a present from Clark! A little thank you after our first movie together!" She chuckled naughtily. "This one's different from all the others though, very special indeed, aren't you my little man?"

She picked up the dog and pressed her carefully painted lips to its toothless mouth. Michael felt quite sick.

"I'll never replace you. Will I, my little darling? You're too special. Mummy loves you too much." She settled the dog on her knee.

Carla entered and placed a silver tray on the table.

"You pour, Michael. The bottle's open. Pass my gin, darling. Isn't this nice? Cosy." She turned her head left and right. "Divine!"

"What amazing glasses!"

"Oh, I'm so glad you like them. Russian, nineteenth century. I do so hate those tall modern flutes. Don't you? Ghastly. Pretentious bourgeois invention. What's the point in bubbles if they don't go up your nose!"

The boy spoke for the second time, in an untypically hesitant way.

"Is it... real Chanel?"

"Oh bless! Sweet. Yes, it is. Couture, of course, darling." She purred. "Nineteen sixty five. Good collection. Very wearable.

Useful little things, just to slip on. Never buy off-the-peg! Well, I do now, occasionally. Can't stand for the fittings. Don't really go anywhere much now anyway. And those new ones are frightfully clever, if you choose carefully. Karan, Armani, Jill Sander. How clever of you to notice. You like clothes? I think we are going to get on. What's this divine little thing? She fingered the boy's ear and threw Michael a look. "A present?"

"Yes it's from Cartier. In Monte Carlo."

It was the first time Michael had seen the boy blush.

She patted the boy's cheek.

"Sweet! Now I'm going to go and start getting ready for dinner. I can't hurry. Not any more." She blew the whistle again. "You stay here and finish your drinks. Oh, by the way do you like my library?" She looked at the boy. "You'll appreciate it if you know about fashion. It's an exact replica of Chanel's salon in her Ritz apartment, Paris. Oh, Carla, I want to go up and start getting ready. Here, carry my drink up for me. Run me a bath.... Please dear." Atlanta turned to Michael. "She lip reads." And back to Carla: "Then come and show the boys up to their room. You have put them in the Aviary haven't you? And do make sure the lift is down dear, you know how I hate standing." She coughed again. "You'll love your room, boys. It's too divine, though I say it myself. Stay and finish your drinks, finish the bottle. Carla will show you your room when you're ready. Make yourselves at home. Anything you want, anything, ask Carla. There's a whistle there in the ashtray, and you'll find a whistle by your bed. She'll hear it even if she's at the other end of the house. It must be the pitch or something. You know like dolphins! Meet me back here at eight-thirty. No need to get

The Butterfly Boy

dressed up. We're just going up to the village, to Gina's. Not smart at all. It's tiny. There are only six tables. Best food for miles. Real Italian home cooking. Gina makes everything herself, from scratch. No menu, you just get whatever she fancies cooking. I know you'll love it."

🦋

"Oh, Michael I simply can't believe this. It's the most beautiful room I've ever seen!" The boy grabbed hold of him and waltzed him around the octagonal bedroom. The Aviary was frescoed with a design which made the whole room appear like the inside of a giant bird cage. Beyond the elaborate painted cage, a blue painted sky was dotted with white fluffy painted clouds. The eight tall windows were draped in white muslin, which was looped back at irregular intervals by the beaks of multi-coloured birds. Michael examined them. They were real birds, stuffed ones!

Hanging from the centre of the domed ceiling, a smaller gilt bird cage, was filled with more brightly coloured birds. Suspended from it's base a veil of white muslin, completely encased a huge circular white bed. Sewn onto the white muslin, in a haphazard fashion, was a multitude of small silk flowers, daisies, violets and primroses, looking incredibly lifelike, as if they had just blown in through the windows on a spring breeze. Three of the seven windows were in fact not windows, but mirrored doors. One disguised the entrance to the room. Another lead into large white marble-lined bath room, and the third into a dressing room. Not only had their suitcases been brought up, but, they discovered, unpacked, and their clothes neatly arranged in the wardrobes and their toiletries carefully set out in the marble bathroom.

"Wow!" exclaimed the boy. "This is what I call service!"

On a gilded table between two of the windows an ice bucket contained another bottle of champagne, obviously just opened, the neck wrapped in a white linen cloth. Michael filled the two glasses.

"I know you won't say no!"

"I won't say no to a shag! We've got time haven't we?"

※

"Give me your arms boys. I hate these steps"

Franco held open the front passenger door of the old white Daimler. Atlanta gingerly got in. She was wearing a silk jersey dress of the darkest navy, the square neck, outlined with a broad border of fine matching suede, punched in a decorative pattern like brogue shoes. A matching band of suede held back her perfect hair do. As Franco arranged her seat belt, she patted his cheek and pushed a stray lock of black hair back from his forehead.

The road was incredibly narrow and winding. Atlanta turned with some difficulty to look at the boy, who sat behind Franco, dressed once more in black.

"Nice isn't it? Jean Muir, darling. Seventy something, can't quite remember exactly. Never dates. A genius, poor darling. Mad as a hatter! Bloody sharp cookie though. Never gave me a penny discount. Went to dinner there once. She made us all

The Butterfly Boy

take our shoes off! Bloody nerve. White painted floors. All very chic, but barking mad!"

Inside the tiny restaurant Gina, a huge woman wearing a floral pinafore over shiny lavender short sleeved sweater and black skirt, greeted Atlanta like a long lost relative. She hugged her so hard Michael was afraid she might snap. They babbled away to each other in Italian, throwing occasional glances at Michael and the boy.

"She's over-excited because she's never had an Australian in her restaurant before, except me! Darling, light me a cigarette."

She handed the boy her small black quilted leather shoulder bag with a gold chain straps.

"She want's to know what Australians eat. Is there anything you don't eat?"

"No, well I don't eat that much red meat. But honestly anything."

Michael looked at the boy.

"Anything at all, I just don't eat huge quantities."

He handed the lit cigarette, in it's holder, to Atlanta.

"Thank you, darling. You don't mind do you?" She looked at Michael.

"Of course not," Michael lied.

The meal was superb. Beginning with a seemingly endless procession of antipasti, first cold then hot. Atlanta ate almost nothing, though she did become very enthusiastic about a plate of thinly sliced wild raw mushrooms, dressed in lemon and olive oil.

Gina hovered around like a clucking hen. Obviously concerned that the boy wasn't eating as much as she thought he should be.

"Darling, don't be bullied. She likes her men fat as pigs. Just taste a tiny bit of everything. Never too young to worry about getting overweight! Although you're perfect darling, at the moment." She patted the boy's hand. "Tomorrow I'll show you my collection. My clothes! Better than any museum! You can choose for me, what to wear tomorrow night. Got to look fabulous. It will be quite a do. Enrico is so chic. Quite funny how we met. We share the same drug dealer!"

Atlanta talked non-stop, regaling them with all kinds of humorous stories and scandalous gossip about her days in Hollywood. As the pasta course arrived she slowed down.

"Darling, not for me. Wheat allergy. But I know it'll be divine. Her own pesto. The best in Liguria. She always makes it at the last minute, while the pasta is boiling. Look it's much chunkier than normal, and I've never seen it served like that with extra pine kernels? Sometimes I just have the pesto on a spoonful of soft polenta, I can eat that. Now enough of me. I want to know all about you two , from the beginning."

🦋

There was a knock on the door next morning at around eight. Michael was just coming out of the bathroom, wrapped in one of the white towelling robes, embroidered with the name Capricci on the pocket, which hung behind the bathroom door. He looked for the boy, to make sure he was decent, before opening the door. The boy was standing outside on the balcony, which ran all around the outside of the room, wearing a plain black cotton sarong, slung around his hips. He was taking photos of the garden.

Carla bobbed a little curtsy to Michael, then carried the large tray out onto the balcony. For the boy, she almost curtsied to the ground. Another adoring fan!

They sat down to the most perfect breakfast. Fresh white peach juice, coffee, warm bread, obviously home made preserves, and, much to the boy's obvious delight, yet another bottle of champagne.

He half-filled two glasses with the peach juice then topped them up with champagne.

"Bellinis! I've read about them in *Vogue Entertaining*. They serve them in Harry's Bar in Venice. They invented them. Oh, I'd love to go to Venice. Can we go, Michael? One day, I mean? You haven't read your note. Open it, I'm dying to know what it says!"

"One day? One day!" Michael thrilled, glowed at those words. One day. It inferred a future! One day out of many. Many days to come! How could anyone be so lucky? He opened the lavender envelope addressed in scrawly spidery writing, in purple ink.

Good morning, darlings

I hope you slept well. Well, not too well!

Michael, I want the boy to myself this morning. You must amuse yourself until lunch time. Take the car if you want. Franco is at your disposal. Imperia's quite interesting. It's just down the road. I'm going to give the boy a lesson in fashion history. You'd be bored stiff. Tell him to come to the library at eleven. You're lunch will be served at one - on the terrace . Go through the library windows.

I'm sure you won't mind me borrowing the boy for a few hours.

Have fun!
Atlanta

Carla was already waiting in the library when the boy arrived. She was wearing the same blouse and cameo brooch, but she had changed the grey skirt for a heavy tartan kilt in dark wintry tones.

"Bonjourno, Signora," the boy mouthed, realising that because of Carla's age and unfortunate appearance, it would be much more flattering to address her as 'Signora' rather than 'Signorina'! His flattering little salutation had the desired effect. Carla flushed visibly and dropped the deepest of curtsies.

He followed her to the lift. She got in after him and closed the black and gold ironwork double gates. The boy drank in the details of the lift. The walls were covered in an intricate marquetry design in the Pompeian Style which was so popular in the Italian Renaissance. It reminded him of photos he had seen of the Raphael Loggia in the Vatican. He noticed from the corner of his eye that Carla, still flushed, kept her head down, apparently examining her sturdy brown lace-up shoes. She smelt strongly of lavender.

The lift stopped on the third floor, and they stepped out into a long gallery-like room which ran the entire length of the back of the villa. It had windows all along one side looking out to the terraced gardens, and against the opposite wall, jutting out into the room, was a seemingly endless row of what turned out to be clothes rails shrouded in tailored white linen protective covers.

"Good morning, darling. I trust that breakfast, and everything else has been to your liking?"

"Good morning. Yes, Oh yes. Thank you. Simply fantastic."

Carla backed into the lift and disappeared. Atlanta was sitting in a vast throne-like gilded armchair, upholstered in what appeared to be real leopard skin, obviously very old and balding in places. By contrast Atlanta was looking almost child-like. She wore a navy blue linen dress, perfectly plain except for a tailored white collar and cuffs in immaculate ribbed cotton pique. It was flat and and tight over the bosom, flaring stiffly out to finish just above the knees. Her incredibly long slender legs were encased in stark white tights and she wore flat navy patent shoes with square toes. A padded navy blue velvet band held back her hair.

"Welcome to my little museum. My own personal slice of history. It's probably the most complete collection of twentieth century fashion. Well, the last half of the century shall we say," she raised her finely arched eyebrows, and chuckled naughtily, "in the world. I've only ever bought the best. It's been my little passion. My obsession. I love people with obsessions. I love to observe them. That's why I find Michael so fascinating."

"Michael?"

"Yes, darling, he doesn't look the sort of person to allow himself to be ruled by an obsession?" Eyebrows raised again.

"Michael?"

"Darling, don't play the little ingenue with me. You know that you have got him completely wrapped around your little finger." She reached out and lightly fingered the diamond earring.

"But..."

"Don't worry, darling. Been there, done that. You don't think I paid for all these!" She tossed her head sideways, indicating the rows of white shrouded shapes. "Well, not in the beginning!"

"But honestly..."

"Shhhhh sweetie. Don't try and explain. You'd be mad not to cash in now. You won't be able to forever." Atlanta gripped the boy's chin with one hand, turning his head this way and that to examine his profile. 'Well, I don't know darling. You certainly have got superb bones. You should be good for quite a few years yet if you look after yourself!"

The boy opened his mouth to speak.

"Enough my darling boy. Schhhh. I love clever people. And I love beautiful people. The two together however, are quite irresistible. Yes, I think you're quite a special boy. Now enough of that, I think it's time to being our little lesson.

"This is nice isn't it? Patou, Jean Patou. I wore it specially because it's the same year as the Chanel I wore yesterday; sixty five, spring/summer. So different. Chalk and cheese! I loved Patou. It was such a fun time for clothes. Courrèges and Ungaro were doing such clever things. Pierre Cardin tried very hard, but never really got it quite right I didn't think. Clever things, they seemed quite wild at the time. But not compared with those crazy young English designers. Mary Quant, Zandra, Ossie Clark, Bill Gibb. They actually started the whole revolution. But, darling. Not for me. As I said I only ever wore couture. Or at least one-offs.

"But Patou was lovely for the times when one didn't want to stand out. Nice little things like this for... lunch, shopping. For smarter occasions I adored Givenchy. But of course for really grand stuff Balenciaga was... well Balenciaga was in class of his own. The master!

"Now take off that cover. That one." She indicated one of the clothes rails. The linen cover was fastened with large mother of pearl buttons. The button holes were hand made, the boy noticed, fingering them lovingly. Atlanta observed his attention to detail and smiled approvingly.

"Sixty to sixty five. See it's embroidered on the end. Most are in five year cycles, unless it was a particularly interesting period, or, I had a particularly rich husband, or protector, at the time.

"Now that's Courrèges. The white one. Take it out. Notice the seams down the front of the trousers. The slits to go over the white boots. Now, to the right. The splash print, after Jackson Pollock, of course, that's Ungaro. So clever. Superb fabric, triple gabardine. Nattier. The best. Everyone was using it. Now look at the seaming, or lack of it. It appears so simple, but to get that shape with so few seams! Those frogs really new how to cut."

"Darling, there's the car. Your lovely boyfriend must be back. I hadn't realised the time. I won't join you for lunch. Well, I never eat lunch, darling. I only get the cook in at lunch time if I've got people. Normally I just have a bowl of Japanese miso soup. It's so good. I get from the health shop in Imperia. It comes in little packets, dehydrated. Just add boiling water. Well, I don't," she laughed. "Carla does. She thinks I'm mad. Now quickly, darling. I must have my rest. It's going to be a big night. What shall I wear? Have you chosen?"

The boy held out a dress from the sixty five to sixty eight rail.

"Oh how funny! What an odd choice! But no, I think it's perfect. Hardly dated! Bit dressy perhaps, but who cares?"

"Who's Thea Porter?"

"Exactly, darling. English actually. Not big league. Not couture of course, but did one offs. Rather arty. Quite fun. All part of that rich hippie bit."

She took the dress from the boy and held it up to the light. It was chiffon, but loose, shaped like a caftan. Long and flowing, it was divided up into three horizontal bands. The top of the dress was a deep dusty pink, the middle was a shade of burnt orange, and the bottom section was exactly the colour of lavender. Not only was the fabric printed with a complicated paisley-type design, but was embroidered all over with multi

The Butterfly Boy

coloured sequins and beads, with a particularly heavily encrusted border which ran around the hem, up the front and around the edge of the flimsy hood which hung down the back of the dress.

"I had to wear it with heels. Not really fashionable at the time, but it was just a teeny bit too long. That's the trouble with not having things made. Couldn't be shortened, because of the embroidery. Stitched straight onto the dress, see?

"Funny story attached to it too! Supposed to be a 'one-off'. Got it for the Oscars. Couldn't believe it, Liz had on exactly the same dress. Well as near as damn it. I walked straight up to her and said 'I hope I look half as good in it as you do.' I did, darling! She was so sweet. Do you know what she did? I got a letter, three days later, through my agent, to say that we were both going to get a full refund! And we did, which was a bit of a hoot, as I'd only paid cost in the first place!" She chuckled naughtily.

"Off you go. Darling, send Carla up when you get down. I've forgotten my whistle. There's one on the silver tray on the table in the entrance hall. Oh, no, of course, you're having lunch on the terrace. Just use the one in the library. Bon appetit. Have a lovely afternoon. We'll meet back on the terrace for some bubbles, or whatever else you fancy, at seven thirty. No, eight o'clock. Don't want to get to the party too early. Don't want to appear too eager. Although I think you'll have fun. All kinds of important people will be there. And lots of beautiful people!" She took the boy's chin in her hand again. "But not many clever, beautiful people!" She chuckled. "Give me a kiss darling."

Richard Cawley

"What do you think, darling? I'd almost forgotten it. It does look rather good doesn't it? Far too long of course, as I said. Can't wear heels now. Won't be doing much walking though. Do you like the bandeau?" She patted her hair. "Poor Carla, I drove her mad looking for something that would go. Colour's perfect isn't it? Bit plain, but there's enough going on in the dress. You look divine, darling, *très* chic."

The boy was dressed in a totally simple fine black linen Mao suit with small round buttons like a row of black currants shining down the front of the jacket. His hair was glossy with wax and arranged in little twisted points all over his head.

"You too, Michael." She proffered her white cheek for a kiss." The skin, Michael noticed, was surprisingly smooth and cool. She smelt of exotic flowers. Jasmine? Gardenias? Michael hadn't worn the cheesecloth shirt since the fashion show.

They all turned as a harsh screech disturbed the quiet of the evening.

"Bloody things!" A peacock strutted across the lawn with its fabulous open tail on display, quivering.

"Some people don't need such ostentatious display." She looked down at her dress, fingering the heavily beaded border and laughed. She looked at the boy, patting his arm, then at Michael with a little knowing smile. "Now let me tell you about Enrico before we set off. You've heard of Capricci? Divine bags. Well everything now, of course, like everyone else, watches, perfume, scarves. But originally, just leather, bags, shoes etc. Well, Enrico *is* Capricci! The sole owner. Filthy rich. It was started by his great, great grandfather, who originally made saddles for the Italian aristocracy. He branched out into trunks and suitcases. In those days everyone travelled by ship. He was so clever. Everyone just had to have their luggage made by Capricci. Well look at it all now. He's got to be one of the richest men in the world, well, Italy anyway. Spends most of his time either in New York, or Milan, where the factories are. He hardly ever comes here in the summer. Usually only or a few days at Christmas. So I suppose this is something to do with the new boyfriend. Actor apparently. Well, singer. Does musicals. Not met him. Supposed to be a stunner. Well, he'd have to be. German. Won't last. They never do. Trades them in at least twice a year. Well, we'll see won't we? Michael pour us all another glass of champagne, darling."

Michael noticed with fascination that all during the forty minute twisting journey up the hillside, Atlanta, who sat with the dog on her knee, rested her heavily bejewelled hand on Franco's beefy thigh. Occasionally the driver would turn his head sideways and give Atlanta what appeared to be a genuinely affectionate glance.

Eventually they drove through a long narrow medieval-looking village with arcaded buildings of dark stone bordering either side of the main street. Just on the outskirts of the village they came to a high forbidding looking new wall of the same dark stone. Franco stopped the car in front of a massive pair of dull silver metal gates, which were covered in an irregular arrangement of shiny pointed metal studs.

Franco got out of the car and pressed a button in a panel to the side of the gate. He then spoke into a slatted grill. The doors slowly and silently swung open to reveal what appeared to be a forest of giant bamboo. Brilliant points of light flashed between the thick yellow and green stems as they drove along and around the dense bamboo hedge to the house.

"Fabulous of course, in its way, but not quite my taste. Still it's only one of his many residences, and you can bet the yacht is moored not far away on the coast, just in case he needs a quick get away! And it is a bit of a contrast to the family home which he now owns. Unbelievable renaissance palazzo in Rome. It covers a whole block, right in the centre. Michael, you'll have to give me your arm."

Franco had opened her door and helped her onto the white marble drive. He then picked up the dog.

"It was designed by de Lucca. You've probably never heard of him. Disciple of Le Corbusier."

The house, although only one story high, appeared vast, and blazed with lights, it being constructed mostly of glass, with supports and details in grey concrete and the same dull silver metal as the gates.

In the centre of the entrance hall, a huge sculpture was the only furniture. A series of thick glass rods, of varying height, rose straight out of the concrete floor. Directly above each rod, a shiny silver sphere was suspended on fine, almost invisible wire. The spheres appeared to hover, a few centimetres above the glass columns. The effect was fabulous. Behind the sculpture, sliding windows led through to a large courtyard, again devoid of any decorations except for a central square pool, lined with dull silver. From the waters rose a similar arrangement of glass rods, but these were obviously hollow, as water

The Butterfly Boy

was trickling down their outsides. Simple fountain jets also shot straight upwards here and there at random, making a pleasant pattering sound. An identical hallway on the opposite side of the courtyard led directly into the gardens.

Atlanta walked very slowly, supporting herself on Michael's arm with one hand, and gingerly lifting the beaded hem of her dress with the other. The boy carried her flame-coloured slub silk bag and walked with confident ease, as if he was totally unimpressed by the obvious grandeur of his surroundings. Michael, who was already apprehensive about meeting the beautiful people, was impressed by the boy's cool composure. Franco walked a few paces behind carrying the dog.

No one seemed to notice as they stepped out onto the warm Travertine marble terrace. The beautiful people seemed totally engrossed in themselves, and each other.

Handsome young boys, no older than fifteen or sixteen, dressed in no more than white ankle length sarongs, moved among the crowds with trays of drinks. One of the boys approached them smiling over the tall flutes of champagne. His short tightly curled blonde hair and china blue eyes gave him an almost angelic look. Straight from a Botticelli painting! Michael thought. The boy fluttered his thick dark lashes at him in a far from subtle manner, as he handed him the third glass from his tray.

"We must find somewhere for Atlanta to sit," the butterfly boy burst out in a rather curt fashion, turning his back rather obviously on the beautiful young waiter. Michael was thrilled to witness this little display of jealousy.

"My dear Atlanta, as chic and beautiful as ever." A deep

voice with a perfect English upper class accent, broke the slight tension of the moment.

"Enrico, you old rogue. Darling, at my age I could hardly be described as beautiful, but I will graciously accept the compliment about being chic." It was Atlanta's turn to flutter eyelashes; false ones. She lowered her head in a mock bashful way.

"Rather good isn't it, the frock? The boy chose it for me." She nodded, smiling towards him. "And this is Michael, from Australia."

Enrico greeted Michael with a courteous shake of the hand and slight bow of the head. He then greeted the boy, obviously studying him carefully, and, Michael observed, holding onto his hand for a fraction of a second longer than was necessary when he shook it. Although Michael was not feeling exactly at ease in such obviously glittering company, he felt oddly confident about the boy's commitment to him, especially after the little scene with the blonde angel!

Enrico took Atlanta's arm from Michael and led her over to one of the reclining chairs which surrounded the spectacular Olympic-sized swimming pool. The lounger was made from steel and canvas, upholstered with deep cushions covered in broad grey and white stripes. Franco gently lowered the dog onto Atlanta's knee, bowed slightly and disappeared back in the direction of the house.

"Michael you sit here with me. I'll fill you in on the people I recognise. We'll speculate on the rest!" She laughed. "Enrico take the boy, I'm sure you want to introduce him to all kinds of influential people! And I'm sure he'd love a guided tour of this fabulous house. And... make sure he has everything he

The Butterfly Boy

needs to really enjoy the evening!" She gave Enrico a barely perceptible knowing look.

Atlanta began to point people out in the crowd, telling Michael who they were and what they did. There were artists and actors, famous plastic surgeons, politicians, mostly middle-aged and expensively but discreetly dressed.

Then there was a much younger crowd, more flamboyantly dressed and all incredibly good looking. Michael saw Enrico stop on the other side of the pool and introduce the boy to a tall blonde stunningly good looking young man.

"That must be his new trick! The *cher*man!" Atlanta scoffed. "Michael, darling, would you be a total sweetie and get me something to eat, I need something to soak up the alcohol."

"Will you be alright?"

"Of course, darling. I've managed all these years. I think I can look after myself for a few minutes more while you get me some food. It's over there I imagine. In that grey tent thing. People seem to be coming from that direction with plates."

Michael picked his way nervously through the crowd. Nobody seemed to give him a second glance, it was almost as if he was invisible, whereas all eyes had turned earlier when the butterfly boy had walked past. He didn't mind, he was more than happy to be an invisible observer.

Yet more boys, slightly older looking ones, were serving the food. There was no choice, simply what appeared to be a mountain of split lobsters, enormous glass bowls of salad, the tiniest of leaves, all green, and smaller white porcelain bowls of thick shiny mayonnaise, flecked with green herbs.

"Oh darling, how divine. He's just so chic, isn't he? The last time I went to one of his parties, all he served was grilled asparagus with shaved parmesan followed by a pea risotto. I got the recipe, for my cook, the stock is made with the pea pods, too divine!

"Michael, darling, as rent for my little French house, you must deal with my lobster. Cut it up for me. I simply can't have my fingers smelling of seafood, darling. It's no problem for you to pop off to the boys' room to wash your hands. Can't have you with fishy fingers can we?" She gave a surprisingly dirty laugh. Michael was shocked, but, he noticed, her words were already sounding a little slurred.

Atlanta ate very little, a few forkfuls. She fed the remainder to the dog, from the heavy, obviously solid silver crested fork, first dipping each chunk of lobster in the mayonnaise. Michael tried hard not to show his revulsion.

"Sweetie. I'm dying for a drink, a proper one. Go and see if you can get me a gin and tonic. A nice big one sweetie. Oh, and darling, if you see Enrico, ask him if he's got one of his special little treats for me. He'll understand."

When Michael got back a few minutes later with Atlanta's gin and tonic, the boy had returned and was sitting at her feet on the end of the lounger, playing with a plate of salad. He looked up at Michael with a beaming smile.

"I made sure they put loads of gin in, but I didn't see Enrico."

"No you wouldn't, the boy added excitedly. "He's just had the most amazing row with Axel. That's his boyfriend. Don't know what it was all about. They were talking in German. He can speak every language under the sun. Perfectly. Even

Japanese! But, oh, the house. It's unbelievable. He's got real Picasso and Braque and Chagal...!"

At that moment Enrico joined them. Only his flushed face showed signs of the recent row.

"Michael, I'm sorry, it is Michael, isn't it? Yes. I need to borrow your young friend again. Someone's just arrived I think he'd like to meet. Eva. She's Dutch. Rough as a truck driver. You should see what she's wearing! But one of the best textile designers around. Unbelievably sensitive work. She does most of our scarves. Funny really! She's known affectionately as the Van Dyke!"

"Atlanta, my darling, when you next need go to the ladies room, use the one next to the cinema. I've instructed Jeanetta to look after you!"

"Oh, darling, how thoughtful. I was beginning to get a little anxious. Didn't bring any of my own. Know how you look after a girl in these matters," she chuckled. "Michael, my darling. What would I do without you? I need to wee-wee anyway. Help me, darling. God, my legs are stiff. Now, darling," she patted the dog, "stay there like a good little pooch. Mummy won't be long."

Michael felt slightly embarrassed waiting alone outside the cloakroom for Atlanta, but she was surprisingly quick. He supported her as she tottered back to the poolside.

"Oh, fuck the little mongrel. Where the fucking hell's he fucked off to?" Atlanta almost screamed as they got back to the lounger.

At that moment, from nowhere there was a sudden strong wind.

"Oh, my god. That means rain. It always does at this time of year. Get me inside. Quick," she snapped at Michael. He was shocked and hurt. She took his arm and started to walk quickly towards the house. Everyone else, obviously used to the local weather was already heading in that direction.

Suddenly there was a violent crack of thunder, and at the same time the garden was illuminated brightly by a lightening fork.

"Fuck, that was close. Where's Gable? He must have smelt it. That's why he's fucked off. The little runt. Hurry let's find Franco. Oh god, no!"

The rain suddenly fell from the skies in a solid heavy sheet. Atlanta scrabbled at Michael's arm as her knees gave way under the sheer weight of the water. She shrieked as a sudden gust of wind forced the torrent sideways. Something pale flashed across Michael's face, whipping and stinging his eyes. He gasped when he looked sideways at Atlanta. Now completely bald, her perfect makeup, running down her face in streaks of black and scarlet. The chiffon dress, heavy with water and embroidery, stuck to her frail shivering body as if it had been sprayed on.

"Come on. Let's get you into the house."

She took one jolting step forward, and fell to her knees. Her foot had caught in the hem of the dress. Michael managed with great difficulty to drag her to her feet. She was now crying and screaming hysterically. The bottom panel of the dress was half ripped away where it joined the middle section, revealing pale elasticated stockings which finished below her swollen knees, one of which was badly grazed and bleeding profusely.

The Butterfly Boy

Somehow Michael managed to get the gibbering wreck of a woman into the house. He could hear laughter and loud music in the distance, but luckily there was no one around to see the shame of this poor sad old woman. She managed to shake a wet hand in the direction of one of the many doorways. Jeanetta, smoking in the half open entrance to the cloakroom, handed Michael her half smoked cigarette, and with motherly little coos and tuts took Atlanta into her own arms. She looked down at the white bald head and then up into Michael's face with a pleading look.

"I'll try." He wondered how he would find Franco. They must get her home.

Outside the rain was still falling steadily, but not as heavily as before. The gardens were totally deserted, except for the debris of plates and glasses rolling this way and that. How would he ever find it, the wig?

Suddenly he saw it, pale, floating right in the middle of the dark swimming pool. "Damn, why can't it be near the edge?" He raised his arms to dive. The narrow wet sleeves of the cheesecloth shirt made it almost impossible. He shivered with cold. He felt incredibly alone. He wished David was there. David would have taken over. David always made everything alright. Before he got sick anyway.

He walked along the edge of the pool until he came to a shiny curved silver rail. He turned round and began to lower himself down the steps. The shirt floated up around his chest. The water felt extraordinarily warm. A slight relief. He turned and swam, breast stroke towards the beige floating mess. He touched it with one hand, then stood up. The water came to his chest. He brought up his other hand to lift the wig from the water. How could it be so heavy? He dropped it immediately. His mouth filled with lobster flavoured vomit.

"Oh, Christ. That's the final straw. I can't tell her."

He lay the dead dog by the side of the pool and walked slowly back towards the brilliantly lit house. A dark figure was silhouetted against the still open garden entrance.

He knew when he saw the boy's face that something was, or already had gone terribly wrong.

"Michael. I don't know how to tell you. It's nothing to do with you. I *do* love you. Honestly I do. It's just that... I'll never get an opportunity again like this. He's going to give me my own label. He's been thinking of branching out into a range of younger clothes for a year. Looking for the right designer. Please try and understand. He wants me to start now. Leave with him tomorrow. I had to say yes. I couldn't say no. Could I?

"Oh, please Michael don't look like that. Say something. Please try and understand. I do love you. You could follow me, in a while, when I've got settled..." The boy's hand went to his ear. "Look, please, I can't keep this. Not now..."

"Keep it, for god's sake. I don't want it. Don't make things worse. Please. Don't say any more."

Michael walked past him into the house, then stopped, staring in front of him.

"How can I have been so stupid?"

"Michael! Please! Wait! Don't just..."

Michael walked off into the house to find Franco.

The Butterfly Boy

He had slept for most of the flight. Kind of numb but not as bad as he expected. The Prozac seemed to help. He was glad he had had the foresight to keep them with him. He watched the baggage start to arrive onto the rubber conveyor belt. His was the second bag off. Well, I suppose I am due for some good luck, he tried to console himself.

He picked up the small canvas bag and headed for the green channel. Carole had been more surprised at his sudden departure than he had anticipated, but had seemed overjoyed at the prospect of being paid to close up the house and ship all his stuff back to Australia.

He opened his mobile.

"Mark, it's me."

"Michael, where are you?"

"At the airport."

"What the hell? Hang on I'll be there."

"No. Don't. It's fine. I'll just jump in a cab."

"But it won't..."

"Honestly Mark. It'll be quicker. I'll be home in less than an hour."

"Are you alright? Are you ill?"

"Yes, no. I'm fine. Honestly. I'm doing pretty bloody well, actually. A bit tired, but really not bad. I'm so looking forward to seeing my old friends. Looking forward to a Scotch. A nice big one!" Michael was surprised to hear himself laughing, particularly as he could feel the tears welling up in his eyes.

He opened the door of his apartment and threw in the canvas bag. There was a huge mound of mail just inside the door. "Later," he said aloud.

The door opposite was open. Mark was standing just inside the doorway. He looked so nice. So safe. So reliable... A feeling of relief began to surge through Michael's tired body.

In the background Michael could hear his favourite Tracy Chapman album playing.

Michael walked towards the welcoming open doorway, smiling through his tears. They flung their arms around each other.

Mark reached over Michael's shoulder and pulled the door to. They clung to each almost violently. Then Mark broke the silence.

"You bastard. Have you any idea how much I've missed you. Shit, I don't actually think I can go on like this any longer!"

Michael could hardly believe what was happening.

Mark clamped his mouth onto Michael's. Their bodies, instantly ignited, began to to melt, fuse together. Breathless, Michael pushed himself away. It was all suddenly so confusing.

"Mark?"

"Oh, fuck it, Michael. It's too late. What have I got to loose now? Don't you know? How can you never have realised?"

"Oh, Mark! I never thought for one moment? How stupid. All this time! Oh, no. Oh, god. Oh, fuck. Of course. If only? Oh, Mark, my wonderful friend. How can I? Oh, shit. Oh, fuck. Oh, god." He gave in. Melted completely.

Tracy Chapman sang: *Words, don't come easily*.

Michael woke up several hours later, smiling. A pair of strong smooth arms held him tightly. Tightly but gently. Mark was still asleep. Michael had never felt so happy, so safe, since...?

He smiled to himself. He thought of Dorothy and the red shoes. How could he have never realised? So much time wasted! He sighed. He needed a pee.

Smiling, he carefully entangled himself, from Mark's arms. He didn't wake. Go and get Mark's present! he told himself. One of the few things he had managed to pack. It was his favourite drawing. He knew Mark would love it. He had always wanted him to take up painting again. He knew exactly where it was, right on top.

Michael dropped to his knees, his body suddenly limp, like a marionette with no strings. His head fell forward, his shoulders jerking violently as he sobbed silently. His glasses slid off his wet nose onto the canvas bag. He heard the door opposite open, but didn't look up. He felt so confused.

"Oh, why can't life be just simple?" he agonised.

"Come on. No more tears. It's all going to be OK now." Big strong hands dragged him to his feet. Decisive, confident arms held him tight.

"Go on then. Cry your heart out, my darling. Just for now. Just this once. Then never again. No one is ever going to hurt you ever again. Don't you see this is where you are meant to be. Where you've always meant to be. Here in my arms. Doesn't it feel right. It's all I've ever wanted. To hold you. To look after you. To protect you. To love you. You've no idea what it's been like all this time... David. And afterwards, I thought perhaps in time... But then that boy! That... No, I mustn't. You're mine now. I've waited long enough. And after last night, I know it's right. It was meant. Oh, Michael. How I love you. I love you so much it hurts. And you love me, I know you do. It'll be OK I promise. No, not OK. Perfect! I'll always be there to look after you now. No more tears. Not ever again."

He took Michael's head in his hands and tilted it upwards.

"Oh, Mark!"

"Shut up!"

He kissed Michael hard on the mouth. Michael felt himself dissolving. The big hand on his back made him quiver. His cock began to harden again. Mark's mouth felt so big. So forceful. So different from... He stopped the thought and let his mind, his body just give in, be overpowered. Momentarily he tried feebly to extricate himself from Mark's embrace, to push himself away. They were in the open doorway and on full view to any passers by after all.

"I was just going to get your pres..."

Mark silenced him with another kiss.

"Later, much later."

They stayed in bed until four in the afternoon, alternately making love, sleeping and talking, only occasionally getting up briefly, to pee or bring back snacks from Mark's immaculate kitchen. At one point, as they were drinking champagne and giggling about crumbs in the bed, Michael suddenly sat bolt upright.

"Oh, Mark, you've missed work!"

"No, I haven't. It's Sunday. And anyway I begin four weeks

holiday tomorrow. I've been thinking..."

"Oh, I thought..."

Mark kissed him.

"I've been thinking. Look this is all pretty important stuff. You and me, I mean. It's too important. We've got to get it right. I think we need some time together to ourselves. We need to get to know each other, all over again. I think we both need to get used to this new situation, before we face Sydney, you know, Damian and everyone. And, anyway, I think we need a honeymoon." He sniggered. "I for one am determined to make up for lost time!" He kissed Michael again, this time long and slow. Michael felt himself dissolving, melting yet again.

He would say yes to anything, he decided. How could he resist? But Mark's next suggestion made him pale, and took his breath away.

"Let's go back to France. Now. Straight away. I had originally planned to come, before... It all sounds so wonderful. I want you to show it to me."

"But."

"But what. That's all over. Your old life. Today is the beginning of your, I mean *our* new life. Let's start as we mean to go on. I'm sure it will be a bit difficult at first, but I think it's like falling off a horse. You have to get straight back in the saddle or you'll never ride again. Anyway, from the way you wrote, you adore that place. You sounded so happy there. Even on your own, before... Anyway I'm too selfish. I want to see it all, the house, the river, to meet your hippie friends, maybe to shock Carole!"

Oh, god... what would Raphaella...? Michael paused and took in a deep breath before he continued - "Look, Mark, you're right, we do need to get adjusted to this new situation, some time together, yes, and Bellejac is the obvious solution. I'm sure I can cope. Start there again. In France. For the third time. But there's just one thing I'm going to ask of you Mark. I'm sure I can explain to everyone, Carole, Pierre and Marie Ange. They'll be cool once I explain. They'll love you." Michael kissed Mark this time. "But Raphaella! She simply wouldn't. I couldn't. Mark, I know it's a bit like guilty teenagers, but I just can't hurt her. We'd just have to make a pretence at separate rooms!"

"Oh, if that's your only condition! We'll just have to make sure we go to bed really early..." Mark laughed.

"I must phone Carole. What time is it?" Michael became quite excited, breathless. "She won't have begun to pack up my stuff yet. And then, what time did you say it was, I'll get straight on to the travel agent. Let's get on the first available flight. If we're going, let's go straight away. Let's get away from Sydney. I don't think I could face anyone yet. Oh, god, no. You need a visa!"

"Got one! I applied for it immediately after you left. Remember Rhyme and I were supposed to visit you? Look, Michael I just can't go without saying good-bye to Rhyme. I thought dinner? You don't have to come. But we could go to the veggie Chinese, for old time's sake. We wouldn't bump into anyone else here."

"No, I'll come. I'd love to see Rhyme. Well. I'd better start making some phone calls, and you'd better start packing!"

Michael didn't know whether it was him, his mood, his poor battered mind had certainly had enough to cope with in the past few days, but something had seemed odd. Not the same. At first, Rhyme had seemed genuinely pleased to see him back. She'd fussed over him and shown him lots of affection. But as the story slowly emerged about him and Mark, Mark had done all the talking, she seemed to withdraw, become distant, cold almost. Then after a while, and a few drinks, she seemed to pull herself together and become almost overly jovial. But it seemed forced, unnatural. As they said goodbye at the end of the evening, she'd promised she was going to follow them to France in a couple of weeks, for a visit, but Michael knew it was a lie.

In the taxi going home, Michael became pensive and silent. He wanted to break the silence, to break the mood, his mood? But he didn't know what to say. He felt it was Mark's turn to speak.

"You OK Michael?" Mark gripped Michael's hand and gave it a squeeze.

"I don't think Rhyme really approves of me any more."

"Don't be stupid Michael. Of course she does… It's just…"

"Just what?"

"Oh shit, it's difficult. It's difficult to explain without sounding like a complete arsehole."

"What, what are you talking about?"

"It's just that… well… Rhyme and I seem to have been pushed together a lot recently. What with you being ill and then..."

"Mark, you haven't?" Michael felt suddenly nauseous, dizzy as if he was going to faint. "I just couldn't, couldn't..."

Mark put his arm around his and dragged his head down onto his shoulder.

"Don't be stupid, Michael. Haven't I made my feelings for you quite clear. Mind you if I had had the tiniest drop of straight blood in me it might have been difficult not to give in."

"What do you mean?"

"Well, to be honest... well, the truth is... Rhyme's got a bit of a thing about me... She thinks she's in love with me."

"Rhyme? But I was becoming more and more convinced *she* was gay?"

"She definitely isn't gay, I can assure you of that!"

"But how...?"

The taxi came to a stop outside the apartment block.

"Eighteen dollars exactly, please."

Michael noticed the cab driver for the first time. She was so fat she had trouble turning round. 'A woman driver. Unusual!' he thought. 'I'm sure I've seen her before?' He couldn't think where, but something about her made him feel uncomfortable.

As soon as the apartment door was closed, Mark grabbed Michael and started to smother him with kisses.

"I'll show you I'm not straight," he laughed.

Suddenly Michael remembered where he had seen the fat woman taxi driver before. The scene flashed before his eyes. He froze, rigid. The art gallery in the background. He could hear her laugh. The boy. The rose...

"Michael, what's the matter?"

"Nothing. Nothing at all." He let his body give in once more. Forced the image from his mind. Let himself be enveloped by Mark's big strong body. It made a wonderful change to be the hunted rather than the hunter. To be overpowered, dominated, adored, lusted after. It seemed that Mark had plenty of lust as well as love, Michael noted as his clothes were being ripped of moments later.

They had sex twice more during the night and Michael was woken early next morning by a hot mouth exploring his body yet again. How often he had woken the boy in exactly the same way... He forced the image from his mind. Fuck the boy, he thought. It's the past. It's over. I'm over him...

"God, you certainly are making up for lost time, Mark. You're not exactly making much allowance for my jet lag!"

"We'll be back in France before you have noticed any jet lag. Shall I stop."

"God, no, don't stop. Oh, shit don't stop now whatever you do."

The hot air hit them like a blast furnace as they stepped over the gangs of squatting back packers outside Avignon station.

"Shall we pick up the hire car and set straight off for Bellejac. It's only an hour."

"You must be joking. You wouldn't come with me to the toilet on the plane for a shag." Mark laughed. "You're certainly not going to whisk me past Avignon when I've never been here before."

Mark certainly was beginning to show Michael a side to his character that he had never seen before. He had never realised how strong and forceful he could be. And the sex thing was certainly a surprise. Michael smiled smugly to himself.

"Come on then I'll take you to our only gay bar."

Avignon was bustling and electric with excitement. The festival d'Avignon was in full swing. Every spare scrap of wall was covered with posters advertising alternative theatrical productions and actors in outrageous costumes paraded through the streets packed with holidaymakers, handing out leaflets. Michael's eyes were taken by a blonde youth in a skimpy white Greek style costume with large white feathered wings. A boy, he noted. Then he turned to look at Mark. His big strong Mark. A man! He sighed with pleasure.

There was one small table left outside the café. Michael began to feel a little nervous as they squeezed their way in. He would have to go straight in and explain the situation to his friends to save any embarrassment. He would leave Mark there. Say he was going inside for a pee. But just as he was about to speak a commotion inside the café distracted him.

"Get out and don't come back. This isn't Marseilles you know." A waiter, one Michael didn't recognise, pushed a figure roughly between the tables and into the road.

"This is the last time. Don't come back. It's hard enough, without your sort."

The man, apparently pretty drunk supported himself,

swaying slightly with both arms outstretched on a litter bin. His head hung down over the bin and he seemed to be cursing to himself. Something made Michael study him. Skinhead hair cut, ripped faded jeans, skin tight white singlet, Celtic tattoo on his arm, muscular arm, good body, he noted.

"Oh god, no!"

Mark caught hold of Michael's arm as he moved towards the drunk.

"You know him?" Mark looked very concerned.

"Yes. I think so." He pulled away from Mark's grip. He put his hands on the man's bare shoulders.

"Bruno. Are you alright?"

Bruno straightened himself up and span round, leaning unsteadily with his bottom against the bin.

"Well, what a surprise. It's the master. It's Monsieur Michael!" His words were slurred, and he spoke with mock respect. His eyes were hazy and bloodshot and his face was filled with contempt. Michael took a step back. He half expected Bruno was going to try and hit him, or at least spit at him.

"Bruno?"

"Oh, Bruno. You remember my name then!"

"Please Bruno. Oh, Bruno, I'm sorry."

"Ha! He's sorry. That's nice. He's sorry. Well what about me. I'm sorry. Very sorry."

One hand gave way and he started to fall. Michael caught his arm to steady him, but Bruno winced and pulled his arm away. The tattoo was obviously quite new and sensitive, Michael noticed. Then he took in a huge intake of breath as it registered. In the centre of the design in a Celtic style script was the letter M.

"Oh Bruno! I know you won't believe me, but I..."

Bruno's face crumpled. The look of hatred completely disappeared. He now looked like a whipped dog. Hurt. Feeble. He started to shake. This time he didn't pull away from Michael's touch. He looked up into his face with large black sad eyes.

"You said you didn't have anyone. You lied!"

"I didn't Bruno. I didn't lie. I really didn't lie. I thought I didn't have anyone. I thought it was all over. That's why I came to France. To escape. To get over it..." He turned to look at Mark's concerned face. "And that one? That's him is it? At least I know it wasn't because I was too old!"

"No that's not the one, he's only... Yes, that is him. We've known each other a long time." Michael felt an instant feeling of relief, when he realised that Bruno had obviously never seen the boy. At least this way, it made it easier.

Bruno shook his head as if to clear his brain and straightened himself up.

"Well, Monsieur Michael..."

"Please don't call me that Bruno. I really....."

"Well, Monsieur Michael, I must at least thank you for what you taught me."

"Taught you?"

"In bed. It comes in very useful. I wouldn't have been able to satisfy my customers..."

"Bruno! You can't! You don't mean it!"

"I most certainly do. Beat's gardening. And markets stalls."

He flashed an obviously brand new Gucci watch in front of Michael's face.

"Please, Bruno!"

"Oh, please is it. Please, Bruno." He sneered again. "Well, I might. For an old customer. If you ever fancy a change from him." He flashed a look over Michael's shoulder." Might even give you discount." His face crumpled again and his eyes filled with tears. "I'm sorry Michael, but I don't think you know..."

"I think I do." He touched the Celtic M. very tenderly and gently. Bruno's hand close over his and gave it a faint squeeze.

"Goodbye, Michael." Bruno turned and walked slowly and surprisingly steadily away, his head hung low on his chest.

"Goodbye Bruno."

Mark caught Michael's arm as he tried to hurry past into the café.

"Give me a minute. I'll explain."

🦋

The next day Michael's heart jumped as he heard the door open. He was waiting, on his own, in the yellow salon. It was the book Mark had given him to read on the plane which had decided him. Feel the fear and do it anyway.

She still had a key.

"I'm in here Raphaella, come and sit down I need to talk to you." If this thing was going to work, if he was going to finally sort his life out, everything had to be out in the open from the word go, he decided. No pretence at separate beds. And if she didn't like it she ... well she would just have to go.

Raphaella sat on the very edge of the tapestry chair, head down, hands folded in her lap and listened without uttering a sound. Michael told her the whole story, David, the boy, Mark, everything.

"Well, Raphaella?"

She paused, silent for a while, and then looked up and spoke.

"It's very difficult for me Monsieur. I have no experience of such things, and... I'm a Catholic.

"I'm not though," Michael smiled gently into Raphaella's concerned face.

"And you're Australian!" Raphaella actually laughed, and took both Michael's hands in hers. "If you're happy, Monsieur Michael!"

He dragged her to her feet, hugging her, lifting her off the ground.

"Oh, I am, Raphaella. You don't know how happy I am. At last, really happy." He put her down and gave her a big hard kiss on the cheek. "I think we both need a little drink now we've got all that out of the way. And, of course, Mark is dying to meet you. He knows all about you. And Raphaella I want you to start calling me Michael, just Michael, not Monsieur Michael."

"A little drink would certainly be welcome Monsieur, and I am longing to meet this Monsieur..... Monsieur Mark, of whom you are so fond, Monsieur. But the last thing Monsieur. No, I simply can't agree to that. It simply wouldn't be proper." She actually grinned.

After that everything could only be easy. Michael and Mark and Raphaella had drunk champagne together and become the best of friends. The rest of the day had been perfect. Michael made lunch which they ate on the terrace and got quite drunk on rose wine. Not too drunk for sex however, and they spent the rest of the afternoon in bed.

After a perfect dinner in the little restaurant in the Place followed by a walk round the village, they sat on the terrace again, under the stars, drinking whiskey. Michael brought a cushion from the house and placed it on the gravel by Mark's chair, then sat with his head on Mark's lap, while they chatted and planned all the things they would do. They fell silent for a while, sipping their whiskeys and wallowing in each other's presence. Then Michael broke the silence. He smiled up into Mark's adoring face.

"Mark."

"Michael." He kissed his forehead.

"I really... god who's that? What time is it in Australia?"

"Oh, leave it. The answer machine's on, isn't it?"

The voice of the answer machine, Michael's voice, rang out quite clearly in the still, warm night air. "Michael is unable to take your call at the moment..."

They laughed in unison. Then they heard the sound of the fax machine.

"I wonder if something's wrong?"

"Oh, leave it."
"No, I'll just..."
"Shall I go for you?"
"No, I'll only be a minute. Here, take my glass."

※

Michael felt surprisingly breathless after running up the stairs. "Perhaps it's the jet lag. Or the whiskey. Too much sex, more like!" He laughed out loud as he tore the single page from the fax machine. He hadn't bothered to turn the light on in the room and walked over to the window to try and read the fax by the light from the terrace. It read:

Wednesday
Michael

It's all gone horribly wrong. I'm coming home. Qantas from Rome.
I arrive at Marseilles midday on Friday. Please meet me.
I've missed you so much.
I love you, Michael.

No signature, just a small drawing of a butterfly.

Michael held the sheet of fax paper to his lips and looked down over it to the figure on the terrace...